CAVE OF FIRE

CAVE OF FIRE

BY
REBECCA KING

MILLS & BOON LIMITED
ETON HOUSE   18–24 PARADISE ROAD
RICHMOND   SURREY   TW9 1SR

First published in Great Britain 1992 by Mills & Boon Limited

© Rebecca King 1992

Australian copyright 1992 Philippine copyright 1992 Large Print edition 1992

ISBN 0 263 13181 5

Set in Times Roman 17 on 18 pt. 16-9211-46697 C

Printed and bound in Great Britain by William Clowes, Beccles, Suffolk.

CHAPTER ONE

'WHY not just lock her up and throw away the key?'

'And feed her on bread and water, you mean?'

'Something like that, yes. That way, she'd come to heel fast enough.'

'My dear boy ——' the grey-haired man shook his head ruefully '—I'm afraid you're out of touch—the good old days are over. Here in England, just as much as in the States, young women don't take very kindly to being locked up—not even by their doting grandfathers.'

His eyes strayed to the framed photograph which stood on the leather-topped desk. The younger man followed his glance.

'That's her, is it?'

'Yes, that's Dany, taken last month on her twenty-first birthday.'

'Hmm.' Picking it up, he studied it with a professional eye. Not his style, of course; carefully posed studio portraiture wasn't exactly his line. But even so...an oval face, wide mouth curving in the beginnings of a smile, and, beneath the shock of red-gold hair, long, dark lashes fringing a pair of huge eyes. Strange colour...almost golden—no, topaz, that was it ... and definitely more than a hint of devilment. Oh, the photographer had done his best ... the slender neck rising from the ruche of white silk, draped fetchingly around her shoulders, the glowing hair in a soft-focus halo, the mouth a little wistful. And yet——

'Well, what do you think of her?'

He slowly replaced the photograph. 'Quite a—distinctive face.'

'Yes, she's always stood out from the crowd. Take a look at this.' Pulling open a drawer in the desk, the older man rummaged through a pile of papers and drew out a long rolled-up scroll which he tossed across. 'Her school photo—see if you can spot her at fifteen.'

The man opened it out, his eyes searching the ranks of well-scrubbed young faces above neat blue shirts and blouses and ties.

'Here she is.' A lean, tanned finger stabbed at a face, the lips curled into an impish smile, the eyes staring straight at the camera from beneath a heavy red-gold fringe. 'No—wait.'

As he looked up, puzzled, his companion laughed. 'Don't worry—she hasn't got a twin. That's Dany as well. She did it for a bet, running along the back row and jumping up at the far end so she's in it twice.' He took back the photograph. 'Hmm. She's still got her eyebrows here, I see.'

A dark brow was raised quizzically. 'You mean she hasn't always had them?'

'Well, she did lose them for a while. She was organising a barbecue for the local Brownie group at the time and somehow managed to use the wrong fuel. The village hall wasn't totally destroyed, though,' he added hastily, but the other man rolled his eyes heavenwards.

'And *this* is the harmless little kid that you want me to act as minder for?' He laughed grimly. 'It sounds to me as though people need protecting from *her.*'

Taking up his glass, he uncoiled himself from the leather chesterfield and went to stand by the study window, looking out at the lawns and shrubbery, the softly rolling Cotswold hills beyond. A scene so quintessentially English—and so different from that of his last meeting with this man, who he knew, without turning, was watching him with anxious eyes.

He stared moodily down into the amber liquid, cradling the glass between his fingers, then his gaze moved to the black and white photograph hanging on the wall. One of his best, Tom had always said... He remembered that day, just the two of them roughing it out there in the Tierranuevan rain forest. Tom Trent, seeking refuge from the starchy life he was normally forced to lead as cultural attaché in the British embassy in Santa Clara; he, for once on a peaceful photographic assignment—for *National Geographic*, he remembered—and insisting on waiting for hours for just the right moment, when the slanting late afternoon shadows would heighten the dark primeval forest stealthily closing in to swallow up that superb pre-Columbian temple. It seemed a long time ago...

He turned slowly back to face the other man, who was still regarding him steadily across the desk.

'No, I'm sorry, Tom, but baby-sitting just isn't my line.'

'You can treat it as a vacation.'

'Minding that little bundle of nitro-glycerine?' He jabbed a finger in the direction of the photograph on the desk. 'Some vacation!'

'But you've just been telling me how long it is since you had a real break from building up that international picture agency of yours back home in Boston.'

'Yeah, it's been hard work,' the other agreed. 'But worth it—highly lucrative.'

'I'm sure,' the older man said drily, his eyes running over the immaculate-casual Ralph Lauren suit, the white silk shirt, the wafer-thin gold Rolex. 'But surely, my boy, after the kind of life you've led, it's just a fraction—er—safe.'

He laughed. 'Maybe, but you can spare me that smooth diplomat's tongue of yours. I'm sorry, Tom, but you really are wasting your time.'

'Now that's a pity. I've never known you turn down a challenge before.'

'Oh, hell.' He raked his fingers through his thick thatch of dark hair. 'You know I'm a push-over for your particular brand of Old English emotional thumbscrews.'

His companion regarded him for a moment. The face tough, hard-planed, the body at the peak of physical condition, as lean and well-muscled as a forest jaguar— and, when provoked, about as mean and unpredictable. You, young man, he thought suddenly, are nobody's, but *no-*

body's push-over. But all he said was, 'Look, at least listen to what I have in mind.'

With a shrug, the younger man dropped his long frame back on to the sofa. 'Right then—five minutes. What the hell's going on—and where does this appalling granddaughter of yours fit in?'

'Nowhere, I hope, but even so ——' He drew a long breath. 'Danielle—Dany's—an only child. Her mother died when she was three, and Philip, my son, when she was thirteen. I retired early from the service to give her a home—though I'm not sure how good a job I've made of it. She's my only grandchild, and I suppose I've rather indulged her.'

'You mean she's a spoilt brat?'

'Not exactly, no. More headstrong, impetuous—always getting herself into scrapes. But a heart of gold,' he added, as the other man grimaced. 'When she got her first job—as a secretarial temp, by the way—she's always hated to be tied down for long ——'

'I know the feeling,' the other put in drily.

'At the end of the first month I found her living on baked beans because she'd given all her wages to some slimy con-artist with a good line in a sick wife and child needing the pure air of Switzerland.'

Well, that fitted. The younger man's eyes went back to the photograph—that wistful mouth, those trusting eyes. She obviously wasn't fit to be out of her play-pen.

'But I really think she's settling down now, since she got engaged.'

'Engaged?' He set down his bourbon abruptly, spilling a few drops on the glass-topped side table, then went on with barely veiled irony, 'Who's the lucky guy?'

'Marcus Clifford—a medieval history don at Balliol College, Oxford. Really, he's an old friend of the family—he's known Dany since she was a child. I was quite surprised when they told me, but I think he's just what she needs—a good steadying influence on her.'

Poor kid. At the thought of that wild, beautiful girl being confined in the stuffy prison cell of an Oxford college, the man felt a slight, wholly unaccustomed twinge of compassion. But then, 'So, what's the problem?'

'Well, she came bursting in here one evening when I was looking through these.' He produced a folder of pictures of pottery, bowls and vases in the shapes of grotesque animals and men, and gold and jade statuettes. 'Mayan—probably from Tierranueva. They were seized by Customs in Miami, but they think these are just the tip of the iceberg.'

'You mean that damned illicit digging is still going on?'

'It's getting worse,' Tom Trent replied sombrely. For a second, his gaze went to the large Sheraton cabinet, with its rows of ceramics, some broken and lovingly restored, and on one shelf a handful of small jade figurines. He caught the other man's eye and laughed. 'Don't worry, it's all legit—bought on the open market. But too much is slipping through, disappearing forever into the secret galleries of un-scrupulous collectors. Anyway, I told Dany all this, and the next I knew she'd announced that she'd stripped her savings bare and was off on one of those tours up-river to the very region in Tierranueva where they think the looting's going on.'

'For God's sake——' the man sounded almost angry '—you don't think the little fool's going to take a look, do you?'

'Well, no, I'm sure not.' But he didn't sound that sure. 'When I asked her why she was suddenly so keen on this trip, all she said was that I'd told her so much about Tierranueva that she wanted to see it for herself.'

His companion frowned. 'Why isn't this fiancé of hers going with her?'

'Well, for one thing, it's right in the middle of his term.'

'So why the hell doesn't he just put his foot down—stop her, I mean?'

'Stop her?' Tom Trent smiled wryly.

'Hmm. And this is where I come in, I suppose. But you realise what you're asking—for me to join up with a group of pampered, well-heeled tourists.' He groaned. 'Oh, God, Tom, you know that's just not my scene. When I travel, I travel alone.'

'Yes, I know that,' replied the other man placatingly.

'Why me, then?'

'She hasn't met you, you know your way round Central America, and, quite simply, in a crisis I trust you better than anyone else I know.'

'Oh, great. Flattery on top of emotional blackmail now.'

'Not that there will be a crisis,' Tom Trent went on hastily. 'Dany need never even suspect there's anyone keeping an eye on her. I know these tours—they tote them round, wrapped in scented cotton wool, and kid them it's the real world. So I honestly can't see her getting anywhere near any trouble.'

Despite his words, though, just for a second the younger man glimpsed very real worry—no, more than that, fear—in his eyes, and thought suddenly, Heaven preserve me from all close emotional ties. Thanks, Tom, he'd say, I appreciate your asking me, but sorry —— And yet, inexorably, his gaze was being drawn once more to the photograph on the desk. That face...that mouth, the lips parted in an almost tremulous smile...and those wonderful topaz eyes... Oh, hell! Exasperatedly, he ran his finger through his black hair once more.

'Look, when does this goddam tour get started?'

'Well—this Thursday, actually.'

'Thursday? But that's two days away. Surely it's too late to get me in on it?'

'No problem. I know the MD of the travel company, and I'm sure he'll get you in in some capacity or other.'

'I'm sure he will,' the younger man agreed ironically. He paused momentarily.

'I somehow know I'm going to regret this, but OK.'

'Great. I knew you wouldn't let me down.'

He held up a deprecating hand. 'No more flattery, please.' Shooting back his cuff, he glanced at his watch and got to his feet. 'Now I really must be going—make my peace with Mandy.'

'Mandy?'

'Yeah.' He flashed a wry grin. 'She thinks she's off to Cannes with me in the morning.'

Trent also stood up. Although he all but topped six feet, the other stood a couple of inches taller as they shook hands.

'Be seeing you, Tom. And don't worry—she'll be fine.'

He was turning to the door, when the other man spoke, his voice all at once strangely diffident.

'By the way, Dany—behind the tough-cookie act she likes to put on—she's really quite vulnerable, you know—emotionally, I mean.'

The younger man regarded him evenly. 'And me, with my love 'em and leave 'em routine, you think I might be tempted to take my baby-minding to—excessive lengths?'

'Something like that, yes.'

The man deliberately let his gaze lock with those marvellous topaz eyes, which gazed unwaveringly back at him. 'Aren't you forgetting that fiancé, waiting in the wings?' he said at last, though more to the photograph than to Trent. Then, 'Don't worry, Tom, I'll get your granddaughter back to you in one piece, I promise.'

Dany screwed the top back on the peach lip-gloss and dropped it into her bag then surveyed herself critically. There was no point in putting on any other make-up— her forehead was already shiny and little pin-heads of perspiration had broken out along her full upper lip.

She dabbed at her face with a tissue. Heavens, it was hot out here—the damp, sauna kind of heat which made her feel tacky all over, even though she'd stepped out of a shower only five minutes ago. And her hair didn't help, hanging on her neck in a heavy red-gold curtain. Impatiently, she gathered it up into a bunch high on the back of her head with a black clip, then pinned the ends in to form a neat chignon. Much better. Marcus always preferred her hair up like this —

Marcus. She looked down at her left hand, at the pretty antique ring with its circle of garnets and seed pearls, which she'd chosen that spring weekend in Oxford, and smiled to herself, the smile faintly shadowed by wistfulness. If only he were here... Nearly all the group were couples, and since they'd left Santa Clara she'd been regretting more and more the impulsive whim which had sent her into the travel agents only days after they'd finally fixed the wedding date...

And of course she'd been a fool to think she'd get within miles of any smuggling. She pulled a wry face at her reflection— she really would have to wean herself off those Frederick Forsyth-Jack Higgins thrillers she'd been addicted to lately. It was just a good thing that Gramps hadn't suspected anything, or he might have insisted on coming with her.

From outside on the long veranda, which ran down this side of the hotel, came loud, cheerful voices. Hastily dropping the towel which she'd wrapped herself in, she pulled on clean white cotton pants and bra—the ones she'd worn earlier, on the final stage of their trip up-river, were wet with sweat—then stepped into the pretty turquoise cotton sundress, bought, like all her clothes, from one of the chain stores near her tiny bedsit, zipped it up and surveyed herself critically again. It certainly set off her slim waist and the full curves of her breasts and hips, the long feminine line of her thighs, yet somehow she was much happier in the jeans and T-shirts and baggy cotton flying suits she'd been wearing each day on this trip. Spraying herself liberally with insect-repellent, she snatched up her bag and slipped out to join the others.

'Dany—come and join us.' As she appeared on the terrace, Mrs Robins, a plump, kindly lady from Wisconsin, stopped fanning herself for a moment and patted the padded bamboo chair beside her. 'Now, honey, what will you have to drink?'

'Oh, a lime juice, please.' When the waiter—Amerindian, like all the hotel staff here in the small riverside town of Fermina—set down her drink, frosting in the warm evening air, she smiled up at him then gratefully sipped it, 'Mm, that's better.'

'Yeah, hot, isn't it?' Mrs Robins grimaced. 'But Jerry tells us it'll be a darn sight hotter once we get out in the jungle.'

'Do I hear someone taking my name in vain?'

At the pleasant New England twang of Jerry Somers, their courier, there was a chorus of 'Evening, Jerry,' from the dozen or so members of the group. Glass in hand, he sauntered across and casually dropped his six-foot-plus frame on to the lounger beside Dany.

On their first 'let's all get to know each other' evening back in the capital, Santa Clara, realising that they were by far the youngest in the group—he must be—what? Somewhere in his early thirties?—she'd worried fleetingly about whether he might have had any thoughts about a holiday romance, so she'd very early on dropped Marcus's name into the conversation. But in fact, like the efficient courier that he was, he'd been perfectly pleasant but really had paid her no more attention than he'd given to any of his other charges.

Even so, as she smiled at him, she caught the meaningful look which passed between Mrs Robins and Mrs Schofield, another plump middle-aged lady, this time from Calgary, and blushed. Then, catching Mr James's cool eyes fixed on her from behind his tinted lenses, she turned scarlet and hastily sat back into the shade of an overhanging hibiscus bush.

She took another long drink of chilled lime and watched her fellow tourists over the rim of her glass. Five middle-aged couples—four from North America, one Swedish—one elderly German spinster, indulging a lifetime's passion for creepy-crawlies, a Mexican, Señor Batista, who was now, at the age of eighty, finally getting round to exploring his own continent after a lifetime of travelling the rest of the world as an international banker, and herself.

Oh, and Mr James. She glanced across at him from under her lashes, and saw that, as usual, he was bent over a notepad. More minutely detailed notes for this travel book he was working on. As she watched, he pushed up his slipping spectacles with an abstracted finger, then went on writing.

When the group had got together back in Santa Clara, her heart had sunk to her trainers, but then she'd reminded herself that you could hardly expect to find many young people on luxury tours like this. In fact, when she first had the idea of coming out here she'd been tempted to do it the hard way, but she knew very well that if she told Marcus and Gramps that she was planning on backpacking round Tierranueva there was no way she'd ever have got on that plane.

'You're very busy, Nicholas.' Mrs Robins leaned across to peer at Mr James's notebook.

'Yes.' He gave her a polite smile. 'The preparatory stage of any book is always the longest, I'm afraid.'

'That other book of yours you were telling us about,' Dany put in. 'I seem to remember seeing you on breakfast-time TV—you know,' as he frowned, 'promoting it.'

'Oh, no, Ms Trent. I'm afraid the kind of book I write doesn't merit being hyped on *chat* shows.' And he turned back to his notes.

Dany's lips tightened. She really didn't know what she'd done to offend him—he wasn't exactly forthcoming with any of them, but for some reason he always seemed to take a particular delight in putting her down. Oh, well, let him get on with it, she thought, and turned to Jerry.

'Is it all fixed? Our two nights out at Xocambo, I mean? I'm really looking forward to seeing those ruined pyramids.'

'I hope so. Although—' running his fingers through his dark hair, he gave her a disarming grin '—I can't guarantee it, with me being such a late replacement for the guy who usually runs this trip.'

'And you're doing very well,' one of the other women put in. 'Isn't he?' And there was a murmur of agreement. Dear Mrs Schofield—Dany suppressed a smile as the woman patted Jerry's hand before adding roguishly, 'You haven't lost any of us yet.'

'Well—thanks.' Jerry's handsome face flushed at the compliment. 'But don't be too premature, ladies and gentlemen. There's still time for us all to get lost out there in the jungle together.'

'Forest.' Mr James's pedantic voice broke through the buzz of slightly uncomfortable laughter.

'How do you mean, Nicholas?' Jerry turned to him in polite enquiry.

'It's forest in Central and South America—if it's jungles you want, I'm afraid you'll have to go to the Indian sub-continent.'

'There you are, folks.' Jerry alone seemed unaware of the sudden embarrassed atmosphere. 'What did I tell you? I'm the new boy here. Thanks, Nicholas, I'll remember that in future.'

Well done, Jerry. Dany flashed him a warm smile. It was an essential part of his stock-in-trade, of course, patiently handling difficult customers, but dealing with someone like Mr James couldn't come easy.

And he'd have his hands full with all of them tomorrow. Her eyes slid from the veranda, through the trailing purple bougainvillaea, past the hotel grounds and the lights of the small riverside town, and suddenly she had to repress a shiver. Beyond the lights, beyond the manicured lawns and carefully controlled beds of hibiscus and canna lilies, there lay an endless green darkness, waiting for them . . .

The *maître d'* appeared in the doorway and Jerry got to his feet. 'Time to eat, folks. And can I remind you that the folk group is coming at ten, so if you'd all like to be in the bar by then . . .'

As the others drifted indoors, Dany suppressed a shamefaced smile. For a moment, her imagination had really got to her. How stupid. Through the open window, she could see candle-light, pink water-lily linen napkins, gleaming silver cutlery. This trip was all so controlled, so—civilised, that even out in the forest on their two-night safari Jerry would make sure they were perfectly safe.

Only she and Mr James were left. He was still bent over his notes, and all at once a spasm of irritation stirred in her. Surely, he was hardly any older than Jerry, and yet— super-dull, super-precise, super-boring, in his neat cream linen suit and with black hair carefully parted—there was something about this man which grated on her.

Suddenly, she had a thoroughly wicked urge to fracture that neat, precise shell and see if there was a real man underneath. Although it went against every grain in her body, she sauntered across to him with a deliberately provocative wiggle, and stood, her knee almost touching his.

'It looks as if we two have been left behind,' she said softly. 'Shall we eat together?'

As he looked up, she smiled at him. That smile, lighting her topaz eyes and curving her full, soft lips, never failed. Until now, she'd never consciously used it, yet couldn't be unaware of its devastating effect on the male psyche.

The appalling Mr James, though, was apparently immune. 'Thank you, but I prefer to eat alone, Ms Trent.'

He waved his notebook at her as though in explanation, then slowly got to his feet and, shoulders slightly stooped, went on into the dining-room without another glance.

Yet another put-down! Dany stared angrily at his retreating back, but then, as her sense of the ridiculous resurfaced, her lips twitched. She'd been far too liberal with that insect repellent earlier; it had certainly been more than effective on Mr Nicholas dry-as-a-stick-insect James. Still smiling wryly, she followed him in.

'Well, I don't know about you folks, but I'm for a lie-down.'

Mrs Schofield, resplendent in beige safari trousers and shirt, set down her coffee-cup and eased herself to her feet. She beamed down at Jerry, sprawled in his wicker chair. 'Thanks, Jerry, it's been a great two days, and we're all going home feeling we really know this jungle now.'

He got up as well. 'Glad you've enjoyed it. And now may I suggest we all follow Mrs Schofield's example and get a siesta? Remember, we leave at five this afternoon to get back to Fermina in time for dinner.'

Dany watched as, firmly but kindly, he shepherded them indoors, then he turned back to her. 'Have you enjoyed it, Dany?'

'Oh, yes, very much.'

He paused, then, 'Perhaps we could have a drink together this evening, when we get back to the hotel. On our own—for five minutes, maybe.'

At his rueful face, she laughed, hesitated, then said, 'That would be nice. Thank you.'

Back in her room, she stood at the window staring out through the half-closed louvres with a feeling of dissatisfaction. Oh, the rest of the party had seemed happy enough with their two jungle—sorry, Mr James—forest 'safaris' plus an evening stroll, closely supervised, of course, by Jerry and a couple of charming Indians, but somehow she'd sensed that, whatever they were seeing, it wasn't the real Central America.

It was as though the whole site—the ruined city, the brand new tourist hotel which had been built beside it, and the forest which lapped it—was scrubbed in disinfectant every night and hygienically cling-wrapped for the next group. And now they were leaving . . .

But not for three hours. Suppose she sneaked out and had a look at those ruins rising through the trees which they'd glimpsed from the top of that temple yesterday? Jerry had told them that there was nothing worth seeing there, as that site hadn't been excavated yet, and anyway they must never move an inch alone. But he need never know . . .

She let herself silently out of the rear door of the hotel, and from there it was only a few yards' sprint to the nearest trees. Once in their shade, she glanced back, but there was no Jerry in hot pursuit, and now, in her olive-green trousers and shirt, her drill hat jammed down tightly over her flame-like hair, she'd be invisible. Taking a deep breath, she clutched her camera tightly and walked off through the bushes . . .

An hour later, she was leaning up against a cotton tree, wiping her forehead with the back of her hand. Her shirt was sticking to her back and little rivulets of sweat trickled down her inner thighs. But she'd done it— oh, she hadn't made it to those ruins, but she had seen just a little of the real forest. A flock of gaudy blue and yellow parrots quarrelling in a jacaranda tree...an endless column of vicious-looking red ants crossing her path—and she'd leapt back, terrified, from a long green snake which had turned out to be a swinging vine.

But now she'd better be getting back, or Jerry would send out search parties for her. She straightened then stopped suddenly, her ears straining. Yes, there it was—the same noise again, and not a soft forest noise. Just for a moment she hesitated, then pushed on through the bushes, but all at once she came to a sudden halt.

Just ahead, a clearing had been hacked from the undergrowth, making a space around some low stone buildings. In the centre was a pyramid, thick creepers still twined around its upper level, and, swarming all over it like insects, were dozens of men—Indians, except for one white man in drill shirt and trousers and a floppy bush hat.

Her heart was beating wildly. Could this be it—the source of those smuggled gold and jade artefacts? Or was it a perfectly legitimate archaeological dig? Surely not. The one thing she knew about archaeology was that it was snail's-pace work, slow and methodical. This pyramid was being torn apart, ruthlessly ripped open to its very heart.

The exultation bubbling in her, Dany lifted her camera and took shot after shot, then began circling stealthily to get an angle directly into the pyramid. A tree branch was in her way. She moved it aside, raised the camera again—and through the view-finder saw a boy, only about seven or eight, straighten, turn and look right at her.

At the same instant, an arm like corded steel snaked round her waist. As her mouth opened in an instinctive scream a hand was clapped over it, and next second she was dragged back, fetching up against a solid, unyielding body.

The man—she could see nothing of him, but it had to be a man—swung her violently round, pushed her through the undergrowth then flung her down into a shallow, dried-up water course behind some scrub bushes. He threw himself down across her, pinning her struggling limbs beneath him so that all she could feel was his heartbeat against her shoulder-blade and that hard-muscled body, every fibre in it as taut as a jaguar about to spring.

She tried to move, protest that he was suffocating her, but the only response was a fierce nudge of an elbow and a hiss in her ear—'Shut up, damn you!'—as running footsteps and voices came near.

She couldn't breathe, red lights flashed in her brain...then, all at once, as the voices receded, the man's grip was slackening and he was easing himself off her. Still dizzy, her heart almost bursting with terror, she turned her head—and looked straight into a pair of jade-green eyes, icy cold. Eyes she'd never seen before—and yet, surely, the rest of the face which surrounded those chilly eyes was strangely familiar.

Dany shook her head in an effort to clear it, then, as he got slowly to his feet, she gave an astonished squeak. 'Mr *James*?'

CHAPTER TWO

'SHUT up, I said.'

The prissy voice had gone, along with the tinted spectacles, neatly parted hair, the slightly stooping shoulders, and in their place had suddenly appeared a completely different man. A man with an unruly thatch of black hair, a lean face, hard-edged, thin-lipped, and a powerful-looking body. And what a body. As she lay at his feet on a bed of dried leaves, Dany's eyes travelled disbelievingly down from the broad shoulders straining against the black polo shirt, across the narrow waist and pelvis and down the strong thighs encased in blue denims to the knee-high boots in soft chestnut leather.

She gulped. 'W-whatever are you doing here, Mr James?'

'What the hell do you think I'm doing?' he replied in a low, savage voice.

'I don't—' Her eyes widened in shock. 'You followed me.'

'No, honey, I was here first.'

'But—but I didn't see you,' she stammered lamely. This new Mr James was difficult to deal with—to put it mildly.

'You weren't meant to,' he said coolly. 'Just thank your lucky stars, lady, that I *am* here—or you'd be carrion by now.'

The terror welled in her again, but somehow she swallowed it down. 'Oh, that's ridiculous.'

'You reckon?' He looked down at her. 'Let's just say I'm grateful it was only a kid who saw you. They've no doubt decided he was imagining things, and are beating hell out of him right now—or I'd be dead meat alongside you.' His lip curled slightly as she shuddered involuntarily. 'Get up.'

Dany went to scramble to her feet, but her legs were refusing to obey her commands, and next moment, with an angry exclamation, he put both hands under her armpits, yanking her unceremoniously to her feet. She leaned against him for a moment to steady herself, her fingers splayed against his chest, feeling the beat of his heart again through the thin cotton. But then he pushed her roughly away.

'Right, let's get out of here.'

Keeping a tight hold of her arm, he steered her through the undergrowth at a speed which left her first breathless and then exhausted. Once, she stumbled against a tree root and without a word he dragged her to her feet again. The entire journey took place in absolute silence, apart from her sobbing breath. The loathsome Mr James, though, she couldn't help but notice, seemed no more ruffled than if he'd been taking a stroll round the block to post a letter.

At the edge of the trees he halted, pulling her up sharply. 'Now you listen to me, Ms Trent. You go straight to your room, you pack your things ready to leave, and you stay in your room until we're called to the jeeps.' A rough shake when she did not reply. 'Do you hear me?'

'Yes, I hear you,' she muttered sullenly. 'And there's no need to break my arm.'

When he released her, she nursed her wrist, seeing the ring of little dusky red marks already puffing up and darkening the delicate skin.

'That's nothing to what I'd like to do to you,' he said grimly.

'But shouldn't we be doing something— about what's going on back there, I mean?'

'You will do *nothing*.'

Her eyes jerked to his face. 'Who *are* you?'

'We've been introduced, haven't we? Mr Nicholas James, of course.' He pulled out the tinted spectacles from his pocket, put them on, and before her startled eyes became the stooped, diffident academic once more.

'No, but who are you—really?'

His face twisted into a humourless smile. 'I believe the usual answer in these circumstances is—a friend. Now, get going— and remember what I told you.'

Oh, yes, sir, no, sir, three bags full, sir. Dany, her legs still slightly unsteady, trudged mutinously back to her room, let herself in and plumped down on the bed, staring at the opposite wall. Had he really saved her from serious trouble back there? If so, she ought to be very grateful—but some people made it difficult, if not downright impossible, to feel gratitude.

Nicholas James... Unwillingly, her mind stayed fixed on him. How could she have been so blind—not to have seen past the stoop, the slightly bumbling gait, those bulging notebooks, to the real man? And the reality was that, far from being harmless, Mr James was really rather terrifying.

Yes, but who was he? He'd said, ironically, that he was a friend, but could she— should she—trust him? He didn't *look* very trustworthy. And he didn't seem in any hurry to do anything about that illicit dig. Had he really understood what was going on—or had he in fact simply seen her sneaking away from the hotel, followed her, and just been playing some melodramatic game at her expense for his own twisted amusement? Anything was possible with him. But she couldn't simply pack her bags and leave—she had to tell somebody what was happening...

Ten minutes later she let herself quietly back into her bedroom, weak with relief that there had been no sound from Nicholas James's room. She'd certainly been right to tell Jerry. He'd been first astonished—and angry, she could tell that, because she'd disobeyed his rules. But then he'd told her that she was a clever girl, and should now leave everything to him.

Her room was almost dark after the late afternoon sunshine shafting into the passage outside. She fumbled for the light-switch but then, as her fingers met an arm, she gave a shriek, which was instantly smothered by a hand. Surely she knew that hand, hard, digging ruthlessly into her soft flesh. The grip slackened a fraction, the bedside lights sprang to life, and —

'What the hell do you think you're doing in my room?' Her voice rose as she jerked away from him. 'You can just get out.'

'Where've you been?' Nicholas James's eyes were like slivers of green ice boring into her.

'Nowhere. At least,' she hastily embroidered the lie, 'just down to the lounge. There was a magazine there I——'

'Don't play games with me.'

'I wouldn't dream——'

'I'll ask you one more time——'

'Oh, go to——'

'One more time—nicely—where you've been.' His voice was very quiet, but all at once the fine hairs at her nape stood on end.

'All right, then. If you must know, I've been to tell Jerry—about what we saw, I mean.'

'You've *what*?'

'And he's taking full responsibility for informing the authorities, so there's no need for you to concern yourself any——'

'You——'

Mr James seemed to be having a slight problem with his voice. Good, she thought with angry satisfaction. Show him that when he says jump not everybody chooses to leap through the nearest hoop.

He drew a deep breath. 'Let's get this straight. You've told Somers that you've seen that tomb-robbing going on?'

'Yes, I have.' For a moment, at his expression, her heart all but stopped beating, but then she tossed back her red-gold hair defiantly. 'So what are you going to do about it? Give me a good thrashing?'

'That, lady, is the least of what I'd like to do to you. You are a stupid, interfering little bitch.'

'Oh!' Dany's temper, already stretched beyond breaking-point, snapped. She drew back her hand, but before the blow could land he seized her wrist, bending it back with contemptuous ease until tears sprang to her eyes. Their faces were inches apart.

'In future—if you have any future, that is,' his hateful voice grated in her ear, 'you will do as I tell you, exactly as I tell you, the instant I tell you. Do I make myself clear, Ms Trent?'

'Perfectly. But let *me* make clear that you've chosen the wrong woman to try your bullying—oh!' The words ended on a little gasp of pain, as he tightened his hold again.

'Ssssh.' He held up a warning finger, and this time she obeyed.

From further along the corridor there came the soft sound of a door closing. She looked into Mr James's face, saw it freeze into watchfulness, the eyes narrowed like a cat's, and felt that superb, steel-honed body so close to her own that their thighs and hips brushed together, tense.

Towing her behind him, he clicked off the lights, went across to the window and opened the louvre a fraction. Over his shoulder she saw a figure, walking rapidly away from the hotel.

'It's only Jerry,' she whispered.

But he swung round on her. 'We're leaving—right now.'

'What do you mean?' She stared up at him blankly.

'Getting out—now. I can't spell it out any more simply—not even for your single brain cell. And before your friendly courier comes back with reinforcements.'

He gave her wrist a jerk, but she planted her feet firmly on the tiled floor.

'I won't move till you tell me what's going on.'

'There isn't time.'

'Then you'll have to carry me.' She folded her arms.

He muttered something under his breath, then, 'What is going on is that you, alone and unaided, have fouled up my one-man surveillance operation.'

'Your——' Dany's jaw sagged. 'You mean——?'

'Yes.' He smiled at her, not a pleasant smile. 'I beat you by a day to that dig—I took a little moonlit stroll last night when you were safely tucked up here. And I confirmed what I already suspected—that your friend Somers is in it, right up to here.' He gestured to his neck.

'J-Jerry?'

'He's the paymaster. No doubt that smart attaché case he's never parted from is stuffed full of crisp new dollar bills.'

'But it's impossible.' She shook her head in bewilderment. 'I don't believe you.'

'Sorry to shatter your illusions. You obviously go for that still-wet-behind-the-ears act of his.'

'I do not *go for* Jerry in any way,' she retorted angrily. 'For one thing, can I remind you that I'm engaged?'

'Maybe it's you that needs reminding of that,' he replied evenly. 'But if you think this Marcus you've been endlessly boring the pants off us with would approve of your making sheep's eyes at that guy, well, I guess that's up to you.'

As Dany sucked in her breath in outrage, he went on, 'I wasn't the only one taking an after-dinner stroll last night, and I was right behind him when he met up with the guy in the bush hat.'

'Do you know him?'

'We've met.' Nicholas James's face, hard before, was like granite. 'He was tearing the guts out of a Mayan temple in Guatemala the last time we—ran into each other.'

'Oh.' But Dany was still eyeing him warily.

'Look.' His voice crackled with impatience, and he took another swift glance through the louvres. 'We'll finish this in a healthier spot. Out here we're at the sharp end—no rich connoisseurs, no slick gallery owners—just men who'd kill you as easily as I swat this fly.' And he brought his hands together in a gesture which turned her stomach. 'You're way out of your league here, Ms Trent.'

'And you aren't, I suppose,' she snapped.

'No, I'm not.'

He moved away once more to the window, and she stared at him resentfully through a screen of black lashes. Arrogance oozed out of him from every pore, from the way he carried himself, the way he looked at her... And he seemed so convincing, but could she really trust him? Not as far as she could throw him, she thought suddenly. And, as he was considerably taller, heavier and larger in every way than her, that wasn't very far.

'Look, I ——' she began, but he cut in roughly.

'Are you coming of your own free will, or do I have to drag you?' He took a threatening step towards her.

'No.' She backed away from him in panic. 'I'm not. For all I know, you're one of the gang. Yes, that's it.' Her eyes darkened in horrified certainty. 'You're kidnapping me!'

She drew in a sharp breath to cry out, but he pulled her against him, muffling her mouth with his hand. She turned her head wildly from side to side, then, as the pressure only increased, bit him, hard. He uttered a four-letter obscenity, withdrew his hand sharply, and, breathing heavily, they regarded one another in the half-light.

'Do you mind not using such language?' Dany said coldly. 'I'm used to having gentlemen around me, and they don't ⸺ '

He gave a harsh laugh. 'Sorry if I offend your delicate sensibilities, sweetheart, but I have a feeling if I spend long in your company that's nothing to what you'll hear. Tom warned me, but even he underestimated just how ⸺ '

'Tom? You mean, Gramps?' Her topaz eyes widened. 'You—you *know* him?'

'I do have that dubious pleasure, yes,' he replied grimly. 'Although when I promised him I'd get his precious granddaughter back to him in one piece, I didn't realise I'd be dealing with quite such a pinbrain.'

'You promised ⸺ ' she said slowly. 'You mean, he sent you to keep guard over me? He didn't trust me?' In spite of herself, her voice trembled.

'To keep out of trouble? Too right he didn't.'

Oh, Gramps, how could you have done this to me? Landed me with this—this loathsome man?

'Though why the hell he couldn't have unloaded the job on to that precious fiancé of yours——'

Because Marcus would be completely lost in a situation like this—but Dany crushed the disloyal thought.

'But if I'm going to keep my word to him, we've got to move—right now.'

He held out a hand—the hand, she saw guiltily, which had a neat double row of teeth marks across the palm.

'All right,' she muttered. 'I'll just finish packing my clothes.'

'Clothes!' He gave a sharp, mirthless laugh. 'Honey, you'll be lucky to get out of this with your skin intact.' He snatched up her shoulder-bag which lay on the bed, and tossed it at her. 'You can bring this, plus your camera.'

She looked round frantically, 'Oh, no. I must have dropped it—when you were dragging me along,' she added resentfully.

He raised his brows sardonically. 'I suppose you want me to go back for it?'

'No, of course I don't. But it would have been evidence.'

He shrugged. 'I'll worry about evidence later. Let's go.'

'But where?'

'I'd like to take one of the jeeps, but this network's so big we wouldn't get ten miles down the road before we ran into a convenient land-slip or had a tyre-burst on a hair-pin bend.'

Dany's feeling of queasiness deepened to nausea. 'S-so we're going by river?'

He shook his head. 'Too slow. And anyway, I might blend nicely into the background, but you, with that hair of yours —— ' His eyes flicked briefly over her. 'No, we'll make for the air strip and just hope there's a plane available.'

'You mean we're going to *fly* out?' Her voice rose to a squeak.

To her surprise, though, instead of biting her head off again, his face suddenly creased into a grin, showing strong white teeth, his green eyes glinting wickedly.

'Pan Am, Club Class, honey—what else?'

'Yes, but——'

'You know something? You talk too much.'

Seizing her by the elbows, he dragged her roughly to him. As she tried to protest, his mouth came down on hers, hard and fierce. She struggled to clamp her lips tightly against him, but she was too late—his lips ruthlessly forced hers wider open, so that his tongue, far from begging for admission, could thrust in to plunder the intense sweetness of her inner mouth.

How dared he? The ice-cold fury raged in her, and yet beneath it something else was flickering through her veins, something which was quite alien to her, hot and dark and terrifying.

When he finally released her, it was as though her whole body, not just her mouth, had been ravished. She clung to him for a moment, her eyes blank, as a violent spasm ran through her. Just for a second, they stared into each other's eyes, then he released her abruptly.

'D-don't you ever do that again!' Dany's breast was still heaving with the effort to breathe, and she panted the words.

'But, sweetheart —— ' he gave her a brief, unrepentant smile '—at least I succeeded in shutting you up—temporarily.'

She was nursing the back of her hand to her poor swollen mouth. 'If my fiancé were here, you wouldn't —— '

'Ah, yes, Medieval Marcus.' As she shot him a baleful glance, he went on, making her wince at the cool contempt in his voice, 'But as I'm here, and he is safely back in Oxford, it's *my* rules you'll obey—and if you don't want a repeat performance maybe you'd just better keep a rein on that tongue of yours. Now, let's get moving.' And soundlessly he opened the door.

The tropical dusk was falling by the time they reached the edge of the air strip—no more than a rough clearing in the trees, created for those tourists who preferred to sample the terrors of the forest via an air-conditioned day trip from the capital. A couple of corrugated iron shacks, already rusting in the humid air, served as arrival and departure lounges, and three single-engined planes stood in a row at one end of the runway—all of them, to Dany's eyes, terrifyingly small.

He brought up sharply, under the shadow of a logwood tree, so that she cannoned into him. Then he stood motionless, his eyes straining through the half-light.

'What is it?' she breathed.

'Just trying to work out which plane to use. The Lockheed, I think.'

'You mean, you're going to *steal* one of them?'

'That's the general idea.'

She swallowed hard. 'C-can you fly?'

He glanced round at her. 'I took a crash course—at least, that's what the instructor called it after I'd ditched his third trainer aircraft in a week. Only kidding,' he added, as she gaped up at him, but then his brief grin vanished. 'Right, let's go.'

Using the trees as cover, they circled the air strip until they were as near as they could get to the planes. Strips of pale yellow light came from half-open windows in the huts, and she could hear pop music on a crackling radio.

Bending low, he raced across the grass, and Dany followed, panting. He climbed on to the wing, then pulled her up behind him, slid open the cabin door and dropped inside, to reappear seconds later.

'OK, we're in business. Come on.' She just had time to feel the jab of pain as the door panel caught her knee, then he pushed her unceremoniously into one of the seats. 'Strap yourself in.'

As she fumbled with her seatbelt, he slid into the pilot's seat, and a moment later the engine coughed, spluttered and roared into life.

Tiny figures appeared in the doorway of the nearest hut and, arms waving, raced towards them. But already the plane was wheeling round and taxiing down the runway, bumping over every crack and rut in the dry earth. It turned and, as Dany's stomach turned somersaults with fear, raced back. There was a final judder and then they were off the ground, clearing the trees and climbing steadily, turning westwards towards a horizon where the sun was setting in a wild blaze of crimson and yellow flames.

He glanced briefly over his shoulder. 'OK?' And Dany, her panic changed all at once, to bubbling exhilaration, smiled back at him.

'OK.'

His eyes fastened on hers for an instant, then he looked down at his watch.

'We should touch down in Santa Clara in just over an hour.'

An hour! He'd inform the police, she'd make a triumphant phone call to Gramps, then a hotel, a glorious, leisurely bath...and tomorrow she'd be off to London, never to see Mr Nicholas James again.

Her eyes rested on the back of his neck, just at the point where a lock of black hair, maybe just a fraction too long, curved round into a half-curl at the nape. Such an endearing little curl... Dany, horrified to discover that her index finger was itching to twine that curl around itself, hastily removed her gaze to the instrument panel.

As she looked, without really paying attention, several things happened at the same time. A red light flashed on, off, then on, staying on this time. She heard a soft curse, the throttle was rammed in, then suddenly, horribly, the cockpit filled with smoke and the plane went into a steep dive. She sat frozen, her fingers gripping on to the seat, as with every split second, while he wrestled with the controls, the dark green forest rushed upwards to meet them.

There was a dreadful grinding noise as branches clawed hungrily at the fuselage, the world turned half upside-down, and then, with a final sickening lurch, they came to rest, tilted forward at an acute angle.

Barely conscious, she lay back in her seat, taking shuddering breaths as the world spun round her. Then she was dimly aware of a figure bending over her, jerking her face up to his.

'Dany, are you all right?' His voice was rough.

'Y-yes, I think so.' Gingerly, she eased her arms and legs and realised that, miraculously, she was still alive. 'What happened?'

'A fire in the engine—and we'd only got the one,' he said briefly. 'Come on—*move*.'

He undid her seatbelt, but she shrank back. 'No—I can't,' she whimpered.

'*Yes*. If there's any fuel left in the tanks, we could go up any second.'

He slid open the door, and, yanking her half to her feet, pulled her out after him on to what remained of the wing. Then, still supporting her, he jumped down and let her slide down his body. Just for a moment, she stood in the comforting security of his arms, then he released his hold, and dragged her away from the fuselage.

They were in a small clearing on a riverbank, the nose of the plane actually buried in the soft mud at the edge of the water. All around, pressing in on them, were the tall forest trees, dark against the sky. If they'd crashed into those trees —

Dany stared up at him, her eyes enormous. 'Y-you saved my life.'

Then, as her mouth went down, she bit her lip and put her hands to her paper-white face. For a second, she almost thought she felt a hand gently caress the top of her head, but next moment his caustic voice told her that she'd imagined it.

'Never mind *your* life, sweetheart—I was pretty occupied saving my own. And now, if you'll just cut out the snivelling, I'll take a look at the damage.' And from his jeans pocket he dug out a wafer-thin torch.

Dany's legs would not support her a moment longer, and she sank down in a huddle on the bank, watching as the slender beam of light roved all over the plane. Finally, he came back and stood over her, shining the torch down at her until she murmured a protest, then he switched it off and darkness sprang up all round them, apart from the pale gleam of the river.

'We were lucky,' he said laconically.

Lucky! Dany felt a crazy laugh rise in her, but somehow crushed it.

'The wings were half ripped off as we came down, so when we landed the fuel tanks were just about empty. Otherwise——'

He left the sentence unfinished, but she felt the nausea rise in her again at the thought of what might have happened.

'You'll be able to mend it, will you—the plane, I mean?'

He laughed mirthlessly. 'You have a touching faith in me, honey. But even if I could, what would we use for fuel—river water?'

'I'm sorry, I'm being stupid.'

'So—what's new?'

'Yes, all right,' she muttered miserably. 'It's just I d-don't seem to be thinking very clearly.' Her head was muzzy, as all the little night sounds around them in the darkness jangled together inside her brain. 'What are we going to do, then?'

Now her teeth were beginning to chatter, so that she could hardly get the words out. From among the trees came a soft rustle, and in her mind's eye she saw the forest jaguar moving stealthily in for the kill. She scrambled to her feet. 'I don't like it here.'

'But didn't I hear you tell that creep Somers only yesterday how you were *so* looking forward to seeing the *real* forest?'

'Oh, shut up, damn you.' She kicked at an invisible tuft of spongy grass at her feet, wishing it were his face. Of all the tricks fate could have played—to put her out here with this hateful man who never, ever missed a chance to put her down.

'Anyway,' the loathed voice went on, 'it's safe enough to sleep in the plane tonight. No one will be out looking for us till daybreak.' And he disappeared back into the cabin, this time leaving her to haul herself up after him.

When, breathless, she joined him, he was on his hands and knees at the rear of the plane. He looked up over his shoulder at her, his green eyes catching the pale torch-light, like a giant cat's on the prowl.

'There's a blanket here. Wrap yourself in it.' He threw it to her—it was similar to those she'd been tempted to buy in Fermina market, and in the fading light its brilliant patterns glowed—then he held up a bottle. 'And here's some of the local white rum—fire water, but bearable, I suppose, in an emergency.' He grimaced slightly with distaste.

'But not as good as bourbon.' The words were out before she could stop them, and he raised his brows.

'So you've been studying me closely, Ms Trent. Good—I like my women to know my tastes.'

'In alcohol, you mean?' More unwise words, and at his slow smile Dany could have bitten off her hasty tongue.

'In—everything.'

'But I'm not your woman,' she retorted, the heat scorching her cheeks.

'Oh, but you are, Ms Trent,' he said silkily, 'at least, for exactly as long as it takes me to extricate us from this lousy mess you've landed us in.'

'*I've* landed us in? You're the one who crashed the plane.'

'Perhaps you'd care to rephrase that. Surely, you mean brought it down in the only bit of clear ground for miles around?'

The icy chill in his voice should have frozen her into silence, but the very fact that she knew he was right only goaded her on.

'If you hadn't taken a plane with a faulty engine——'

'Oh, I'm so sorry. I completely forgot to give it a twenty-point safety check before take-off.' The savage sarcasm dripped acid on her raw nerve-endings. 'And can I remind you that we're only here because of your bone-headed stupidity?'

'If you feel like that, I'm amazed you don't just walk off and leave me.'

'Don't tempt me, honey ——'

'And don't keep calling me *honey* in that snide voice.'

'Or I might do just that—honey. I don't care for company, yours least of all.' He looked at her for a moment, exactly as though she had crawled out of the river on slimy paws. But then, 'Look, we've both had enough for one day. You detest me ——'

'I certainly do.'

'And I—well, let's just say the feeling's entirely mutual. So we'll back off each other, shall we?'

'Suits me,' Dany muttered, inwardly relieved that he'd called a halt to this edgy bickering. For out of the drab but safe chrysalis that had been Mr James had burst this man, who was a total enigma to her. All that she did sense, very clearly, in spite of her limited experience of the species, was that he was very rough, very tough—and extremely dangerous.

Unscrewing the top of the rum bottle, he held it out to her. 'Get some of this down you.'

'No, thank you,' she said stiffly.

He jerked the bottle, splashing a few drops on her hand. 'Drink it.'

Uncoiling himself, he stood over her and, too weak to risk provoking his anger again, but promising herself secretly that never again after tonight would she lie down under his bullying treatment, she obediently took a couple of sips, gasping as the raw liquor all but peeled the skin off her throat. She handed the bottle back to him.

'Thanks.' He took half a dozen gulps, then screwed on the top. 'You'd better settle down.'

'Do you mean sleep?' she said. 'But I'm not tired.' Whether it was the aftershock—or close proximity to him—she couldn't be sure, but her brain was pinging with tension.

'Do you have any other ideas, then?' he asked smoothly, and, furious with herself, Dany turned away, scarlet-faced.

He was obviously the kind of man who saw every woman as a sexual challenge. Even when he'd just crash-landed a plane and only just emerged with his life, he still couldn't resist baiting her. Marcus never indulged in such would-be macho behaviour—in fact, he'd not put any sexual pressures on her at all, which was one reason why she felt so secure with him. This man, though—was she going to be able to handle him quite so easily?

But when she gave him a sidelong glance she saw that his lips had tightened into an expression of distaste. Maybe he too was angry with himself for indulging in sexual sparring with her—or, no, it was far more likely, as he'd just told her, that he simply couldn't stand her.

Silently, she began cocooning herself in the blanket, but then stopped. 'Are there any more?'

'I don't see any. Why—are you cold?'

'No—for you.'

'I'll be all right.' His voice was very formal now. 'But thanks anyway.'

In the confined space, they were very close. She could feel his warm breath on her face, smell the faint aroma of soap and, beneath that, the intense maleness of him. She ran the tip of her tongue round her lips, which were suddenly dry.

'Well, I'll—er—settle down, then.' And gingerly she lowered herself on to the hard metal floor behind the seats.

He bent over her. 'Here, I've found this empty rucksack. You can use it as a pillow.'

He stuffed it behind her head then stood looking down at her, illuminating her in the thin thread of light. He was only a darker bulk against the pale interior of the plane.

When he at last turned away, she heard the faint crickle of leather as he lowered himself on to one of the seats. She yawned and her eyes began to close as fatigue all at once caught up with her.

'Well, goodnight, Mr James.'

'Make it Nick. I think maybe we ought to dispense with Mr James from now on.'

Of course, she should have guessed. 'You mean it isn't your real name?'

'Well, yes and no.'

And just what did he mean by that? 'So why that Mr James act? Are you some kind of undercover agent?'

She heard his soft laugh. 'Good heavens, no.'

'Well, why, then?'

'When your grandfather sweet-talked me into this, I thought I might as well relieve the—uh—boredom of baby-minding by doing a bit of sussing out on my own account.'

'But you obviously know your way around out here in the forest.'

'Maybe that's because I've spent so much time here. If you must know, Ms Curiosity Trent, I used to work as a photo-journalist, specialising in war photography. I covered most of the fighting in Central America over a period of ten years, before I gave up.'

'Why did you? Give it up, I mean.'

'You ask too many questions.' His tone definitely discouraged further conversation, but something more than mere curiosity was driving Dany further into the minefield.

'You finally realised how dangerous it was, I suppose.'

He was silent for a moment, then, 'There was that, yes. But I think the real reason was that I finally had to admit to myself that my one-man mission to save the world by showing people just how obscene war is was doomed to failure. I'd forgotten one thing, you see.'

'What was that?'

'Human nature.'

'That's a very cynical point of view.'

'Is it? If you'd seen as much of the dark side of humanity as I have, you might feel the same.' He stopped abruptly, but Dany could almost feel the shadows of things— terrible things which he'd captured through his lens—brush across her spine. 'But don't let it worry you,' he went on, his voice suddenly hardening with undisguised contempt. 'When I get you out of this you'll be able to scuttle off safely into Medieval

Marcus's ivory tower and never come out into the real world again.'

'You don't know Marcus,' she protested hotly. 'You know nothing about his life.'

'I can guess.'

'Yes, well——' She ought to put this vile man well and truly in his place, tell him that Marcus was worth ten of him, but somehow she was just too tired. So instead she contented herself with saying tightly, 'Anyway, you still haven't told me your real name.'

'Nicholas James Devlin.'

'Nicholas James Dev——' she repeated, then her eyes flew open and she sat bolt upright. 'You mean, you're Nick Devlin?'

'That's right, ma'am—for my sins.'

'*The* Nick Devlin?'

'Is there another?' His casual arrogance all but took her breath away.

'But I've read about you in the gossip columns—a different girl hanging on your arm every week.'

'Oh, but you shouldn't believe everything you read in the papers, Ms Trent. I

distinctly remember—who was it now?—
anyway, she lasted all of a fortnight.'

In the darkness, Dany surreptitiously
folded the fingers of her right hand over
her left, covering Marcus's ring—though
whether she was protecting it, or it was
protecting her, she wasn't at all sure.

'Well, let's just get one thing straight,'
she said coldly. 'I may be stuck here with
you, but you're not practising your wom-
anising on me.'

'Honey,' his lazy voice licked round her,
'who needs practice?' Dany's fingers tightened over the ring until it cut into her skin.
'But there's no need for you to lie awake
fretting. When I agreed to take on this job,
I told Tom that, from everything I'd heard
about you, you were definitely not my
type.'

'Well, that's a weight off my mind,' she
retorted.

'And on our brief acquaintance I've seen
nothing to make me change my opinion. In
fact, the way you reacted to that one kiss

back there was enough to tell me I was right.'

'H-how do you mean?' she asked uncertainly.

'You see, sweetheart, I prefer my women to be just that—all woman.'

CHAPTER THREE

A PALE light was filtering across her face. Dany rolled awkwardly on to her back, frowned for a moment in puzzlement at the hotel ceiling, which had changed overnight into a barrel-shaped metal vault, then, as realisation came flooding back, she slowly sat up, nursing her neck.

'Nick,' she whispered softly, 'are you awake?'

But there was no reply—he must still be asleep. When she got up, though, stooping in the confined space, she saw that the seat he'd hunched himself into was empty. She bent to touch it and the upholstery was cold. He'd gone—he'd done what he'd threatened and left her!

She stood stock still, black terror welling up in her. Of course, she should have known—last night he'd as good as told her he was the 'love 'em and leave 'em' type.

73

Well, he'd certainly abandoned her with no preliminaries—and no compunction either, she thought bitterly.

The plane door was open. She perched on the sill then let herself drop, landing on all fours on the soft ground, and cautiously straightened up. In the pre-dawn light a faint mist was rising from the river, so that the trees and bushes which grew at its edge seemed to be floating free. From all round her came noises—faint scrabblings, furtive rustlings—which made her mouth go dry.

Then, from a little way downstream, came louder, splashing sounds. Keeping her fear on a tight leash, she pushed her way through the lush undergrowth, and then her heart all but sang for joy. Nick hadn't left her after all. He'd been bathing in the river and now he was wading out. She took a step forward but then all at once stood very still for, as he rose through the milky, waist-high mist, the light glinted on his skin, turning it to marble, and she realised that he was naked. His lithe, muscled body was as superb as a Greek statue—and intensely masculine.

Powerless to move, she stared at him, the blood thumping in her ears, but then, as he reached the bank, somehow she willed herself to turn, fleeing back blindly through the bushes to the clearing.

She heard him come sauntering towards her, and looked up reluctantly from her intent scrutiny of a large iridescent beetle at her feet to see him fastening his leather belt, his black polo shirt slung carelessly across one shoulder, which still gleamed damply. His hair was ruffled, tiny pearls of river water glinting in it, and suddenly she had a powerful urge to run her fingers through that untidy shock of hair.

'What's the matter?' He must have been watching her closely, seen the faint tremor which had run through her.

'Nothing. At least, I—I've got a stiff neck.'

'Here, let me loosen it up for you.'

Tossing down his shirt, he moved behind her, but she shrank away, unwilling all at once for those long, cool fingers to come in contact with her skin.

'No, please, I'll be all right.'

'Don't be stupid,' he said roughly. 'We've got a load to carry, and I don't intend doing my Everest-porter act while you stroll along behind with your hands in your pockets.'

'Oh, of course.' She gave a bitter little laugh. '*So* sorry. I thought you actually cared just a fraction that I can hardly move my neck, but I should have known better. What a fool I am.'

'Yes, you are,' he replied succinctly, and before she could take evading action he pushed her—fairly gently—down on to the bank and, hunkering down on his haunches behind her, began probing her stiff muscles.

'You're trembling. What's the matter now?'

'Well——' she swallowed '—it's just that when I woke up I thought you'd gone.' Of course, that wasn't the reason for the quivers which were running through her whole body, but far better that he should just think she was a coward.

He laughed softly. 'Now, honey, would I do that?'

'I don't know. Probably,' she muttered, but he just laughed again, his breath curling warmly round her nape, as his fingers went on kneading her neck muscles.

'You've got these really knotted up,' he said. 'Undo your shirt so I can get at them properly.'

'No.' Dany clutched the drill shirt to her.

'Oh, for heaven's sake, don't come over all prudish on me now. Undo it.'

Slowly, Dany undid one button, cursing the impulse that had led her the previous afternoon to slip off her bra for coolness before plunging into the forest.

'And another.' He tugged at the collar. 'And another.'

Impatiently, he pulled the shirt down to her elbows, but then, as his fingers brushed against the outer curves of her breasts, his hands stilled abruptly.

'OK, that's enough,' he said curtly, and his searching fingers gently—surprisingly gently—began to move into the little knotted muscles, easing out the kinks.

'Right, is that better?' he asked at last, and she wriggled her shoulders experimentally.

'Yes—yes, it is. Thank you, Nick.'

Still kneeling, she half turned to smile at him, overbalanced, and fell heavily against him. Her shirt slipped even further and her full breasts dragged across his satiny skin, slowly, so that she felt the pull of the crisp, dark little hairs sprinkled across his chest. For a long moment, as he steadied them, they stared into each other's eyes, the first rays of sunlight gilding their faces, then abruptly he jack-knifed to his feet, pulling her up with him.

'Do yourself up.' As she fumbled with the buttons, her fingers clumsy with embarrassment, he went on brusquely, 'I want to put as much ground as I can between us and this thing.' He jerked his head at the plane, but then, as she began to walk away down the bank, 'And where the hell do you think you're off to?'

'I shan't be long, I promise,' she replied placatingly.

He caught her up in two strides. 'I said, where the hell are you going?'

'To wash, of course.' This time, she scowled up at him. 'I'm filthy and sweaty, so —— '

'You'll have to wait—if you wanted a wash, you should have got up earlier. I told you, we're getting out of here.'

'Oh, for goodness' sake,' she burst out. 'It's hardly daylight yet, and I've told you, I won't be long.'

'And *I've* told you —— ' Nick's voice too was rising steadily '—you will just have to stay dirty. If I don't object to you like that, you needn't.'

As Dany stuck her chin in the air and took a determined step past him, he muttered an oath then picked her up bodily and carried her back along the bank, dumping her by the plane. Just as he set her down she kicked his ankle hard out of sheer frustration, and he winced, then put his hands up, one each side of her, imprisoning her against the fuselage.

'For the last and final time, Ms Trent——' she could tell that he was only keeping his voice level with a huge effort '——you will do as I tell you, when I tell you. You can wash later. I want to check through the plane, see if there's anything we can use. It may have escaped your notice, but we have no food. I can live off the forest, but I'm not sure how you'd make out on a diet of grilled iguana and snake stew.' Ugh. In spite of her determination not to let him get to her, Dany shuddered. 'And if you wash, I'll have to waste valuable time minding you.'

She stared at him. 'Minding me? What on earth for?'

He quirked a dark eyebrow. 'So you wouldn't object to sharing your bath tub with piranhas, leeches and crocs?'

He was only trying to frighten her. 'You seemed to be enjoying *your* bathe,' she said coldly. 'And I didn't notice any——' But then she broke off, the poppy-red burning in her cheeks as, too late, she realised what she'd said.

'Well, well.' He looked down at her, a faintly sardonic smile tugging at the thin mouth. 'I didn't realise I had anyone— minding me.'

'Oh, you needn't worry,' she snapped. 'I didn't exactly stay around ogling you.' But she was still hot with embarrassment, so hurried on, 'Anyway, I still don't think it's fair.'

'Fairness has nothing to do with it, I'm afraid, my sweet,' he said coldly. 'In a situation like this, one person gives the orders, one person takes them.' He paused. 'Do I make myself clear?'

'Crystal-clear.'

'So you can wipe that tight-assed expression off your face.' He expelled a long breath. 'Normally, I'm an easygoing sort of a guy——'

'Really?' Dany enquired super-politely.

'Yes, really—the easiest-going guy in the western hemisphere. Whereas *you* are an extremely provoking young woman, and you're having a terrible effect on my amiable nature.'

'You—amiable?' she choked.

'And what's more, you're not fit to be out of your baby-buggy alone.'

'Well, of all the ——'

'But if you want to try your hand out there, well—Santa Clara is about a hundred miles that-a-way.' He gestured towards the green wall of forest pressing in on them. 'Not that I'm heading in that direction myself, of course.'

She gaped at him. 'You're not?'

He shook his head. 'Not with two mountain ranges in the way. OK for flying over—not so good for walking.'

'Where are you going, then?'

'The border.'

'And how far's that?'

'Oh, about six days' hard walking, I reckon—that's at *my* pace, of course.'

'Of course.' Six days... a week, perhaps. How could she possibly stand a whole week in close proximity with this man?

'So...' his even tone left her in no doubt that he knew exactly what she had been thinking '...if you'd rather take your chance with me, you stay in line. Any objections?'

'Plenty.' She glared up at him, but then, meeting his glittering jade eyes, she lowered her head. 'No. No objections. And —— ' it was being dragged out of her with red-hot pincers '—I'm sorry. I know I've been acting like a fool ever since yesterday.'

'Why stop at yesterday?'

His contempt flicked round her like a whiplash and her lips tightened. Typical Nick Devlin, she thought resentfully. Heaven knew it was hard enough to force her lips to frame the word 'sorry' to this man, so why did he have to throw it back in her face? And she didn't need him to tell her how stupid she was being. Of course she had to stick with him—just as close as one of those horrible leeches he'd threatened her with—for somehow she knew that, arrogant, overbearing bully that he was, of all the men in Central America he was the one to get her safely out of this, past jaguars, snakes, crocodiles——

She shuddered convulsively, then next moment felt herself pulled roughly into his arms.

'Don't be scared, Dany. I've told you I promised Tom that, come hell or high water, I'd get you back to him.'

'But—aren't you frightened?' she whispered into his bare chest, and heard his grim laugh.

'Surrounded by a thousand square miles of virgin Central American forest? Sweetie, I'd be a fool if I wasn't scared half to death, but——' his voice shook suspiciously for a moment '—with a tough little red-gold fireball alongside me, I have a feeling that the local wildlife will be more than happy to keep their distance.'

He held her at arm's length, looking down at her, that wicked laughter still glinting in his eyes. 'All right?'

'Yes, thank you.'

He nodded. 'OK, let's have a look-see inside.' And, as she watched, he swung himself up on to the shattered fuselage and disappeared through the door.

Now that it was full daylight, Dany could take in the crumpled sardine tin that had once been a plane, and her eyes darkened in horror as the realisation hit her squarely of exactly how lucky they were to be alive—or rather, how lucky she'd been to have Nick Devlin as pilot, for surely very few men could have safely brought down that crippled craft.

Oh, they were miles from safety, but even so, as she felt the morning sun on her face and the breeze stirring her hair, a rush of joy, of intense gladness just to be alive, which she'd never felt before, rippled through her so that her heels lifted slightly.

'Are you coming or not?'

The caustic voice from the depths of the plane roused her, and she scrambled up and in through the door. Nick was down on his haunches in the small cargo area at the rear, where tins of food were already piled into heaps. Over his shoulder, he slanted her a brief smile.

'You're in luck. Looks as if you won't have to develop a liking for iguana, after all.'

Dany squatted down beside him and took up a couple of the tins. 'Pork and beans . . . and savoury rice.' She looked up at him in puzzlement. 'What are these doing here?'

He shrugged. 'Emergency rations? Or maybe it's supplies for the hotel.'

'But we didn't have food like this.'

'Well,' he said irritably, 'just be grateful. And we'll probably be glad of this, too,' he added, gesturing towards a small box with a red cross and the words 'First Aid' on the lid. Turning to a long wooden crate, he prised off the top, then gave a low whistle. 'Well, well.'

Dany, peering over his shoulder, saw a stack of tools—spades, axes and, their blades glinting in the half-dark, lethal-looking machetes.

'More emergency kit?' she queried.

'Yeah, I guess so,' he replied, although he didn't sound wholly convinced.

Taking out one of the machetes, he made a slicing gesture with it so that the air whistled, then he tossed it down alongside the food. 'This one'll do, I think.'

'We'll have to pay for all this,' Dany pointed out. She was running her finger gingerly along the blade, and now she drew it back sharply, a small gout of blood on the end.

'For God's sake, leave this thing alone, will you? And you can take that prissy look off your face—of course we'll pay for anything we take.' And he turned back to yet another box.

'And the plane. We must——' she began, then broke off as she heard him sharply suck in his breath.

'I don't somehow think we'll be paying a cent for the plane,' he said softly. 'I reckon it belongs to those looters.'

'H-how do you know that?'

'We've struck gold, honey.' He turned round slowly, and she saw, balanced on his palm, and gleaming in the half-light, a beautiful golden figurine. 'Here.'

He held it out to her, and she took it, with slightly unsteady hands. It was a woman, seated cross-legged, holding in one hand a head of Indian corn, while resting on her lap lay a swaddled baby. Her whole body, especially the belly, was grotesquely fat, yet beneath the feathered head-dress the face, with its remote, other-worldly expression, was strangely haunting.

Dany ran the tip of her finger down the curve of one softly glowing shoulder. 'What is it?'

'At a guess, a goddess of fertility—maize in one hand, child in the other. Yeah, that'll be it. A few years ago I photographed a lady very like her that'd been dug up in the Yucatan.'

As she watched, her eyes enormous, he lifted out another cloth-wrapped bundle. This time, it was a huge pottery bowl, with strange, terrifying animals' heads modelled in relief around its rim. Other bowls followed, together with goblets and jugs, some inlaid with intricate patterns, and then, from another package, a dozen or so tiny golden butterflies. He dropped one, almost weightless, into her palm, and she stared at him, speechless.

'When the last Aztec ruler was held hostage in Mexico by the *conquistadores*,' he said quietly, 'they demanded for ransom that an entire room should be filled with gold. Among the things his subjects brought were hundreds of beaten-gold butterflies.'

He gave a rather shaken laugh, and for a moment Dany glimpsed behind the hard cynicism a quite unexpected humanity. Next moment, though, it was gone.

'I think that's the lot.' He was rummaging around in the crate. 'No, there's something else here.'

He parted the cloth and from his fingers spilled a golden chain, from which hung a carved animal's head. Reaching across, he moved her hair aside and dropped the chain around her neck. It fell, cold and heavy, against her flesh, the head swinging softly between her breasts, and when she lifted it up she saw that it was a perfectly formed golden jaguar's mask, the lips just parting in a menacing snarl, the eyes two tiny chips of pale green jade.

She stared down at it for a moment. 'It's wonderful, isn't it?' she said huskily.

'Yes, it is.' There was a constrained note in his voice, and she glanced up sharply into those other jade-green eyes. But then he turned and began quickly re-wrapping the treasures.

'What are you going to do with them?' she asked. 'Are we taking them with us?'

'We've got enough to carry already.' The last butterflies disappeared rapidly back into their bundle as he spoke, and he straightened up.

'Don't forget this.' She put up her hands to undo the necklace.

'Leave it—we'll need something as evidence. But I'll bury the rest.'

He selected a spade, and between them they lifted the box out on to the ground, then he stood looking around him, frowning. 'That'll do.' He pointed towards a big feathery clump of bamboo on the edge of the clearing.

'But isn't it too near? I mean, if they find this place —— '

'I don't intend them to,' he said grimly. 'But if they do, well, *they* would never leave this stuff—and it won't occur to them that we have. And even if it does, they'll go off into the trees looking for it, not right under their noses.'

He was methodically slicing away the turf, then digging out the soft earth. Dany leaned against a tree-trunk, watching him. In the full sunlight, the dark stubble of his beard showed up, giving him a dishevelled, faintly endearing look, quite at odds with his tough personality.

'What's the matter with you?' He glanced up suddenly, and she realised that she had been smiling down at him inanely.

She coloured deeply, then blurted out, 'Oh—I was just thinking how you need a shave.'

'Ah, but surely I'm even more irresistible with designer stubble.'

She stared at him, quite unable to find anything to say. Just for a moment their eyes locked, then his lips tightened in an angry little grimace and he took a vicious stab at a clod of earth.

'I don't suppose Medieval Marcus ever goes a morning without a shave,' he remarked, without looking at her.

'No, he doesn't—and I'd be grateful if you didn't keep calling him that,' she replied tartly, glad all the same to be back safely on hostile territory. This way, she knew where she was, she thought suddenly—it was when, just occasionally, she strayed off it that the ground felt uncertain beneath her feet...

Nick replaced the last turf and tamped it down. 'That should do it.'

'But suppose no one ever finds them again?'

'From the last instrument reading before things went haywire, I've got a pretty good idea of where we are. Otherwise, in a hundred years from now, maybe some

Indians will come across them and marvel how they got here.'

'But they won't know that we two buried them.'

She rested her grubby hands on the earth for a moment, and he laughed ironically. 'Don't tell me you're getting philosophical, Ms Trent.'

He replaced the spade in the plane, then reappeared with the machete. 'Right, now for a spot of camouflage.' He gestured towards a clump of palms. 'Drag those dead fronds across.' Then, going towards the nearest bushes, he stripped off his shirt and began hacking off branches.

Dany piled up the fronds then drew the back of her hand across her temple. Ten minutes' work and the sweat was streaming from her. If only she could take *her* shirt off, she thought resentfully, glancing across towards Nick. His back was to her, and just beneath the satiny, sweat-slicked skin she could see the muscles moving rhythmically as he wielded the machete with seemingly effortless ease. That gleaming skin, the rhythm of the muscles, the blade flashing in the early morning sunlight—suddenly it all set up a pattern in her brain which blurred and shifted, until a wave of dizziness swept through her and her breathing became shallow and rapid. Then, just as abruptly, the pattern was broken as he threw down the machete so that its point entered the earth and it stood quivering.

As he began dragging across the branches Dany pulled herself together and went to help, spreading them over the fuselage until finally he stood back. 'That should do it—from the air, at least.'

He went back into the plane one final time, then dropped out the loaded rucksack, together with her blanket, now neatly rolled around more of the tins and knotted with a rough loop at each end.

He leapt down beside her. 'Think you can manage that?'

Gingerly, Dany picked up the improvised backpack, then hastily let it fall again. Heavens, it weighed a ton. But then, conscious of a pair of sardonic green eyes, she set her chin. 'Yes, of course. Oh, but my bag.'

'It's inside.'

Picking up his own, obviously much heavier rucksack, Nick swung it up on to his back, then stood watching as she awkwardly fumbled herself into the loops. Through her dishevelled fringe, she caught sight of one chestnut leather toe-cap tapping out an impatient tattoo. There was something about that toe-cap...

'So sorry to keep you waiting.' And, when he gave an infinitesimal shrug, 'I suppose you prefer to travel alone.'

'That's right, honey—no encumbrances,' he agreed smoothly. 'A man travels faster that way.'

And turning, he snatched up his machete, then plunged into the green depths of the forest.

CHAPTER FOUR

'RIGHT—hold it.'

Nick stopped so abruptly that Dany, who for the last two hours had been grimly plodding along behind him, head down, oblivious to everything beyond the throbbing pain in her heel and the sweat trickling down her back, cannoned into him. Hastily, she backed off with a muttered apology.

He eased off his rucksack and stood flexing his shoulders as she shook herself free of her pack and let it fall to the ground.

'Neck OK?'

'Yes.' She was almost too numb with exhaustion to speak.

'Good.' But he barely glanced at her. 'You stay here while I have a look round. Sounds like water ahead.'

When he had gone, thrusting his way through the undergrowth, Dany's legs finally did what they had been threatening all afternoon. They turned into jelly and she folded up on to a tuft of spiky grass, where she lay on her back, gazing up at the forest canopy. Just above her head, a host of sapphire-winged butterflies danced in a shaft of sunlight, while just a few feet away from her two tiny hummingbirds, like shimmering gleams of silver and veridian, plunged in ecstasy into the scarlet flowers of a hibiscus bush, sending the nectar dripping to the ground. Wherever you looked there was so much life, so much vitality. The currents of energy pulsated around her, all but visible, making the air twang softly, almost frighteningly.

'Up you get.'

Jolted from her reverie, she jerked her head up, saw Nick standing over her, hands on hips, and thought suddenly, And this man has exactly the same kind of energy as the forest, raw and intense, as though he carries his own field of electricity around with him—and that's why I'm afraid of him, just as I fear the forest.

She got stiffly to her feet. 'Are we going on?'

'Do you want to?' He raised his brows enquiringly.

Dany desperately *wanted* to sound enthusiastic at the prospect of another ten miles, but her, 'Of course,' came out as a feeble croak.

His thin lips tugged briefly into a half-smile, then he picked up her pack and his own and swung off through the trees without another word.

She followed him, the sound of running water louder in her ears each minute, finally parted a clump of bamboo fronds, stepped out on to springy grass, then stood motionless, her mouth dropping open in wonderment. Just ahead, a stream came tumbling over a lip of white limestone from among the trees above them and fell sheer into a deep circular pool before cascading away down the hillside. A fine mist hung in the air and under it ferns and flowering plants grew luxuriantly around the water's edge.

On the far bank, more hibiscus bushes were growing, and among them, its long, white-starred branches arching down into the water, was a huge stephanotis. Dany's brain reeled as she caught the intoxicating perfume of those white, waxy blossoms.

'Oh, Nick, it—it's wonderful.'

She swung round on him, a dazzled smile on her face, and saw that he was watching her. There was something in the intensity of that silent regard that made her tense instinctively. For the length of one flurried heartbeat it was as if something dangerous, which lay like a sleeping serpent between them, had stirred. Next moment, though, his face was as withdrawn and expressionless as ever.

'You approve of my camp site, then?'

'Oh, yes, it's fine.' Somehow, she forced her voice to be as cool and offhand as his.

'That's good.' His tone was underscored with faint irony. 'We Devlins always strive to give—complete satisfaction.'

So he was back on that track again. But then, as her lips tightened, he unhooked a small silver knife from his belt, unclasped it to reveal a tiny can-opener, and tossed it across to her. She just managed to catch it.

'Open what you like—I don't mind what we eat.' As she gaped at him, he added casually, 'And make it cold. I'm not risking a fire tonight.'

'What—now?' Her voice rose. 'But I want to wash.' And her eyes went yearningly towards that cool, limpid green water.

'Oh, for——' He muttered something under his breath. 'Don't start that again. You can spend the entire night wallowing in there——' he gestured with his head towards the pool '——but right now I'm hungry. So you can organise something while I take another look round. You need to eat in this climate, and we've hardly had anything all day.'

'Don't I know it,' she retorted. 'I just had time to snatch a couple of those little fruits off that tree.'

'Yes, but you're learning, aren't you?' he replied silkily. 'You came when I told you to.'

'Oh, you just——'

Dany, holding the penknife as if she would very much like to plunge it into someone's vitals, went across to his rucksack and, snatching it open, began rooting through the tins, trying to ignore him totally. Even so, out of the corner of her eye she could see a pair of long legs, still standing there, and when she glared round at him she caught the tail end of a tiny smile. That smile did it.

'Tell me,' she said through her teeth, 'are you anti-women in general, or is it just me?'

'Oh, women are all very well—in their place.'

She scowled at a tin of spaghetti rings. 'And that's tied to the kitchen stove, I suppose—cave-woman style.' She gave a haughty toss of her red-gold mane. 'I should have known. Typical male——'

He gave her a lazy smile. 'No, not the kitchen. Actually, it was another room altogether I had in mind.'

And as her eyes jerked up to meet his he turned on his heel, leaving her, pink-faced, to burrow deeper into the rucksack.

By the time he came back, she had placed two large flattish stones on the turf beside the pool and, in between them, the open tin of savoury rice together with another, of frankfurters. His hands were full of small rosy fruit, which he heaped on the grass.

'Hi.' Dany, never able to keep up a hate for long, smiled at him uncertainly. 'Sorry about the lack of table napkins.'

'Yeah, well.' Unexpectedly, he grinned, showing those strong white teeth. 'Somehow, I never was very happy with those pink water-lilies. But maybe this will help.'

He reached out from his rucksack the bottle of white rum and set it down beside the fruit.

'This is your chair?' He pointed to one of the stones. 'Allow me.' And with a flourish he pulled it back for her to sit down, before coiling himself on to the other one.

'No knives and forks either, I'm afraid, but I thought we could use these to scoop out the rice.' She handed him a shiny stephanotis leaf. 'It works quite well—look.' And she dug out a mouthful.

He eyed the rice dubiously. 'Maybe I'll start with a frank.' Hooking out a sausage, he took a bite then grimaced.

'I thought all Americans liked them.'

'Sure—sizzling hot in a toasted bun with barbecue relish.'

'Oh, don't.'

She groaned then laughed, and he said suddenly, 'Do you know, you have the tiniest dimple when you laugh—right there.'

And, reaching across, he touched one corner of her mouth. It was only the faintest of finger brushes, and he withdrew his hand immediately, yet it had set up the strangest sensations in her, and left her skin tingling, as though from a blow. She stared at him blankly as, head bent, he took another bite of frankfurter, then she hastily dug out another mouthful of rice...

'Had enough?'

'Yes, thanks.' Dany licked the last of the star-apple juice off her fingers and sat back. 'They're really quite nice.'

He shrugged. 'Not my favourite tropical fruit.'

'Well, no. I prefer pineapples, or—no, mangoes. They're wonderful—that smooth, scented skin, that gorgeous honey sweetness inside. Mmm.' She closed her eyes. 'I could drown in them.'

'You know something, Ms Trent?' he said softly. 'You are a sensualist.'

Dany opened her eyes and she stared at him. She wasn't altogether sure what a sensualist was, but she felt instinctively that it was something she really shouldn't be when Nick Devlin was within range.

'And that,' he went on, his voice still an insidious murmur, 'sounds more like Danielle Trent than any mango I've ever met. You know,' he explained, as she looked at him in puzzlement, 'a smooth, scented skin, and that gorgeous honey sweetness inside.'

'Oh.' She gave a little gasp and hastily bent forward, so that her swinging hair screened her face. 'Nick,' she said in a low voice, 'I—I wish you wouldn't say things like that.'

'Why not? Oh——' his voice hardened all of a sudden '——because of Medieval Marcus, I suppose.'

'No—at least, yes.' But it wasn't because of Marcus. Rather that, out here, the overpowering lushness of the forest was having a very peculiar effect on her senses. And with Nick in this kind of unpredictable mood she was afraid of him. No, far worse than that—she was afraid of her own reaction to him. But she mustn't let him even begin to suspect the effect he was having.

'Anyway...' pulling a face, she got to her feet '...I don't think I smell very sweet just now. So I think I'll wash—that's if you have no objection, of course,' she added tartly.

'None whatever. Fancy some fire-water first?'

He uncorked the bottle and held it out to her, but she shook her head. He shrugged and took a long gulp himself, grimacing as it went down.

'Well, I'll get on with it, then,' she said, but still stood, uncertainly fingering the top button of her shirt before finally going across to the pool. She rolled up her sleeves, knelt down at the edge and began splashing water on to her face and arms. It was heavenly—so cool and invigorating—but it wasn't really enough.

'What the hell are you up to now?'

Nick's lazy drawl made her jerk round. He was leaning back, hands clasped behind his head, watching her from beneath hooded eyelids.

'You said you'd have to guard me if I went in,' she replied.

'So that's it.' That low, hateful laugh. 'But if I don't object to you indulging in a bit of skinny-dipping, I don't see why you——'

'No—I'm fine now.'

She leapt to her feet again and began rolling down her sleeves, but in an instant he was beside her, his hand firmly on her wrist.

'All right, Ms Trent, message received.' He gave her a rather odd little smile. 'You can go in there quite happily. I've sussed it out already, and I promise you there are no crocs—or leeches—lying in wait, not even for your delectable little body. So, be my guest.' And he deliberately turned his back on her and began to busy himself re-packing the rucksack.

Dany stood, gnawing on her underlip and fidgeting with the gold chain round her neck, her eyes fixed on Nick's back. But then, all at once, quite unable to withstand the lure of the pool a second longer, she tore off the chain, then in fumbling haste her shirt, trainers, socks, jeans and panties, and slid down the bank and into the water. As it closed around her sweaty, dust-caked body like cool silk, she gave a tiny whimper of pure pleasure. On the surface of the water were hundreds of fallen stephanotis flowers, and she picked them up in handfuls, crushing them to release their still-potent scent.

Finally she struck out from the side and swam the width of the pool in half a dozen languid strokes, fetching up against the ledge of rock, where she trod water, letting the cascade flow all over her head and shoulders, washing all the grit out of her hair.

She put her face up to the sun, laughing with the sheer joy of it, then froze as she saw, standing on the bank, Nick. With a little gasp, she ducked down further into the water and yelled, 'Go away!'

'Thought you might like this.'

He held something up and, peering through her lashes, beaded with water droplets, she saw —

'Soap! Oh, Nick, where did you get that?'

'Found it in the plane while you were cooing over the gold. Want me to soap your back for you? I've been told I have a very—er—light touch.'

'No—just go away.' She glared up at him resentfully. Why did he have to spoil everything?

He spread his hands regretfully. 'OK—your loss. Here.' He tossed the soap down to her then, as he went to turn away, he stopped, peeled off his black T-shirt and dropped it on the grass. 'Dry yourself on this. Pity I don't have a bath-towel, though—I could have patted you dry then wrapped you in it.'

His voice had sunk to an intimate purr, and just for a moment, before she could take a hold of her treacherous mind, it showed Dany a picture—a picture of Nick, kneeling in front of a fire, holding a bath-sheet, then coming towards her as she emerged from a scented tub, enfolding her in it, and then —

Dany swallowed hard. 'Thanks.' Somehow, she kept her voice expressionless. 'But I can dry off with my own shirt.'

'I've told you—use this.' He nudged the T-shirt with the toe of his boot. 'And then you can wash it for me.'

Well, of all the nerve. He could wash his own T-shirt—dozens of them, if he wanted to. On the other hand, though, he was standing on the bank, hands on jeans-encased hips, scowling down at her, while she wasn't exactly in the strongest position to defy him . . . But if she let him bully her now . . .

'*Please*,' she said through her teeth, and when he raised one brow she went on, 'Wash it for me, *please*, Dany.'

'Hm.' He eyed her thoughtfully. 'I had got one or two other things I wanted to do—checking for jaguar tracks and so on—but I suppose I can wash the shirt instead.'

'All right, all right, I'll wash your damned shirt,' she snarled, then hurled at his departing back, 'But you needn't think I'm going to make a habit of it.'

She glowered at that back until it disappeared among the trees, then, clutching the tablet of coarse white soap, lathered her hair and body all over, with as much pleasure as if it had been her favourite jasmine-scented brand. Finally, she swam back, hauled herself out and picked up the black T-shirt. It was still warm from Nick's body, and as she took it in her hands there came from it the scent that was uniquely Nick Devlin—faint sweat and, beneath that, the vibrant maleness of the man.

Dany stared down at it for a long moment, those strange sensations churning inside her, then began rubbing her wet arms with it fiercely, as though she wanted to scrub her skin away, and with it those unnerving feelings. It was all the fault of this horrible forest—the lushness, the overripeness everywhere, which was having such a potent effect on her senses. Yes, that was it—really, it was nothing to do with Nick Devlin.

After all, he'd shown his true feelings for her clearly enough, hadn't he? *I prefer my women to be just that—all woman...* That was what he really thought of her—and far better for him to feel that way. Certainly, she felt much safer with him in that mood, tossing casually cruel insults at her, than when he was indulging himself with that equally casual, sexual knee-jerk reaction, which, in a handsome, virile man, must be automatically provoked by any woman unlucky enough to stray into his path...

When he returned, machete in one hand, a bundle of tree branches, sharpened at one end, in the other, she was back in her trousers and had wrapped herself securely in the rough blanket. She was just laying out in the sun their two shirts with her white cotton panties, but when she heard his footsteps she turned, then winced.

'What's wrong?'

'Oh, I've got a blister on my heel. The water numbed it, but now it's —— '

'Sit down and let me look.'

'No, I'm all right.'

She went to hobble past him, but he seized her by the elbows and swung her round. 'Sit down, I said.' She hesitated then dropped down on to the grass. 'Which foot?'

'This one.'

She parted the folds of blanket with her big toe and stuck a pink foot out a couple of inches. Taking it in both his hands, he drew it out, tilting it, then gave a horrified exclamation, and when she looked down she saw on the heel a huge swelling, inflamed and oozing gently. Anaesthetised first by fatigue, then by the chill water, she had barely been aware of it for hours. Now, though, the throbbing pain was shooting up her leg, and when Nick—very gently—touched the hot skin she winced again and tears sprang up in her eyes.

'Sorry.' He looked up at her with a rueful smile then flicked off a tear from her lashes with his little finger.

'What a strange kid you are,' he said softly. 'For the first two hours this morning you did nothing but moan about mosquitoes until I found you that repellent in the first-aid kit. And then, when that howler monkey started up right behind you—well, you all but squawked your head off.' He rolled his eyes at the memory. 'But you've said not one word about this. It's those bloody stupid trainers of yours!'

He sounded angry, and to try to lighten his mood she asked, 'What would you have done if you'd known—carried me on your back?'

'If necessary, yes,' he replied grimly. 'Don't move.'

Going across to his rucksack, he fetched out some antiseptic cream, cotton wool and a roll of gauze. She watched as his long brown fingers deftly undid a length then he sliced through it with his penknife.

In spite of her determination not to flinch, Dany tensed as he applied the cream, and he glanced up sharply. 'Am I hurting you?'

'N-no.' She managed a smile. 'You're a very good nurse.'

'I don't think so.' He pulled a face. 'I lack a grain of the essential virtue—patience.'

She watched as he covered the wound with cotton wool then began winding gauze around it. His hair was flopping over his face and he brushed it away impatiently with the back of his hand. He looked tired—no, more than that, strained—the hard planes of his face set into rigid lines, his mouth compressed, as though he were holding himself on an over-tight rein. And suddenly Dany wanted to run her hands gently over his face, to feel the taut muscles relax under her fingers——

The black lashes lifted abruptly and the green eyes stared up into hers. Just for a moment, the forest sounds faded away and that coiled, slumbering serpent between them seemed to stir again and hiss softly. Then, just as abruptly, he sat back on his heels.

'That should do it.' He knotted the gauze, sheathed his knife and hooked it on to his belt.

'Thank you.' Her voice was not quite steady.

'We'll see how it is in the morning. We can always hole up here for a day.'

Dany was horrified. 'Oh, no, I'll be all right. We must get on, in case the looters...' But her voice tailed off, for even as she spoke she knew in herself that it was not fear of any pursuit that was driving her on; rather, it was the need to reach the border, to be safely out of this forest—and away from Nick Devlin.

She eased on her socks and trainers and stood up carefully. Looking around her, she saw that while Nick had been seeing to her foot the sun had slid unnoticed down the sky, casting long violet shadows across the pool.

He picked up the two shirts and felt them both. 'You can't wear this—it's still damp. Mine's bone dry, so sleep in that.'

'But what about you?'

'No problem. I always sleep in the raw anyway.'

'Oh, I see.'

He gave her a crooked smile. 'Don't worry. Maybe out here —— ' he gestured to the surrounding forest, darkening now with the swift tropical dusk '—I might just compromise and keep my jeans on.' The shirt landed at her feet. 'Put it on while I fix somewhere to sleep.'

Scooping up the sticks he had cut earlier, he leapt the stream and began thrusting them into the ground in two parallel rows beside the clump of hibiscus. Dany watched him for a moment then, turning her back, dropped the blanket and wriggled quickly into his shirt. By the time she looked again one much longer branch had been formed into a roof pole, smaller, leafy ones had been swiftly plaited in between, and the makeshift bivouac was complete.

'Your penthouse suite awaits you, madam.' And before she could move he had snatched up the blanket, then her, in his arms, and was carrying her back across the stream. Her head rested neatly in the crook of his neck and shoulder, and beneath his bare chest she could feel the steady rhythm of his heart against her own flurried breathing.

He set her down on her feet, then held her away from him, looking down at her, his face now just a pale blur against the indigo sky. 'Sleep well, Dany.'

She stared up at him. 'But where are you sleeping?'

'Oh, I'll back up against that mahoe tree over there. Don't worry, I've slept in worse places than this.' His teeth gleamed. 'Remind me to tell you some time about the night I slept in that no-star sleaze-pit of a hotel in Cartagena—the censored version, of course.'

She cleared her throat. No, Dany, her inner self was shrieking in her ear, you mustn't do it—you really mustn't.

'You can sleep with me. I mean —— ' she could have bitten off her clumsy tongue '—you can share the blanket.'

'No.'

'*Yes*. I've got your shirt, and it gets very cold at night, so don't be a fool.'

'It's you who is the fool,' he said roughly.

'Why? There's no problem, surely,' she replied with a hint of asperity. 'You don't even like me.'

'Honey, liking has nothing to do with it,' he said wryly, 'After all, I'm only human.'

'Oh.' Through the half-darkness, she felt her skin warm at his words, and then, to her horror, beneath the thin cotton of his T-shirt, her nipples stirred and tautened. 'If —— ' she began huskily, and cleared her throat again '—if you don't sleep here, I shan't either.'

He gave a soft, rather wry laugh. 'You, Ms Trent, are a thoroughly wilful, disobedient —— '

'So you've told me. Well?'

'OK. But maybe I ought to put the machete between us. After all,' he went on drily, 'I seem to remember reading somewhere that in the old days, if a virtuous maiden just happened to find herself sharing a bed with a man, a naked sword between them was the best way of keeping her that way. And you, of course, fully intend to save yourself for Medieval Marcus, don't you?'

Dany's lips tightened. What an arrogant swine he was—and why did he have to put Marcus down at every opportunity?

'Oh, there's no need to worry,' she retorted. 'You see, I prefer my men to be just that—all man.'

He laughed lazily. 'Now that, Ms Trent, sounds remarkably like a challenge.'

'Does it? Well, it wasn't meant to.'

'Ah, well, in that case, I needn't be at all frightened, need I? Now, you settle yourself down—I'm going to wash.'

Dany crawled into the low shelter and curled into one half of the blanket. Her sense of hearing intensified by the darkness, she heard Nick walk to the edge of the pool, then two long 'zizzes' as he undid his boots, another as he unzipped his jeans, and a soft rustle as he stepped out of them and his briefs. Then finally she caught the ripple as he lowered himself into the water.

A few minutes later she heard him again, hauling himself out on to the bank, and without warning the image came into her mind of that morning, that superb, perfectly sculpted body rising through the mist. She squeezed her eyes shut, frantically trying to blot out the picture, to replace it with Marcus's smiling face, but his image was only fragments in her mind—fragments which refused to blend together.

Panic-stricken, she tried to draw Marcus's shadowy form towards her. But then, at another sound, her eyes flew open and she saw Nick, darkly silhouetted against the sky, coming down on his haunches to ease himself in beside her.

'Have you got enough blanket?' His voice was neutral.

'Yes.' She could only trust herself to say the one syllable.

'Well, goodnight, then.' And he rolled on his side away from her.

'Night.' She yawned and felt a little of the tautness leave her, then she sniffed. In the warm darkness, a rich, heady perfume was encircling her.

'Oh—the stephanotis.' She sniffed again, filling her lungs with it, so that the molecules of perfume seemed to travel through every vein in her body. 'Mmm, it's wonderful. I bought one for my bedsit last winter—just a little one in a pot, but it filled the whole room with its scent.'

'Is it still going strong?'

'I don't know,' she said sadly. 'I gave it away to someone I was working with.'

'Why, when you like them so much?'

'Well,' she replied reluctantly, wishing she'd never got into this, 'Marcus didn't like the smell. It gave him a headache, so every time he came to see me he complained.'

'Ah.' That was all Nick said, but there was a wealth of meaning in that single word, and she felt constrained to leap to Marcus's defence.

'He couldn't help it. Some people come out in a rash if they eat one strawberry.'

'So they do,' he replied blandly.

'And Gramps was telling me once—oh, Gramps!' All today, she hadn't spared her grandfather a single thought, and now the guilt shot through her. 'Do you think he knows yet—about our going missing, I mean?'

In her sudden agitation she sat bolt upright, her hair brushing against the leafy roof, and Nick rolled over to face her. 'I doubt it.'

'Yes, but he'll be worried sick if ——' She broke off, her lips quivering.

A hand closed tightly over hers. 'I'm sure that swine Somers won't want anyone starting up a full-scale search for us—they might get to that plane before he does. If I know that bastard he'll have spun some tale about us two staying on to join up with another group. Right now, he's probably dropping heavy hints about an instant romance.'

'Between me and that nice Mr James, you mean?'

'Of course.' He gave a low, throaty growl. 'If you ask me, that Mr James had hidden depths.'

She laughed rather shakily. 'Oh, I'm sure he had.'

'But in any case, just suppose Tom does get to know, he won't worry. He'll know you're safe—you're with me.'

Safe! Nick surely would keep her safe from the dangers which lurked unseen beyond their flimsy shelter. He, if anyone could, would keep those forest jaguars at bay. With her free hand, she clutched instinctively at the gold chain round her neck, with its snarling jaguar mask... And yet safe was not a word which sprang to mind when Nick Devlin was around. Vibrant, yes. Unpredictable, yes. And dangerous— he exuded danger from every pore...

Furtively, she withdrew her hand from his and lay down again in a rigid line, then for a long time, she stared up through the interlaced branches at the diamond points of a million stars, and listened to the steady, rhythmic breathing of the man beside her...

She had been bathing in the pool. Now she stood, naked, at its side, gripped with a primeval fear, for out there in the darkness of the forest something was prowling—something predatory, something feral. She knew she should stay in the open, where she was safe, but inexorably she was being drawn into the trees. She stumbled blindly among them, then tripped over a root and fell headlong, so that she lay dazed.

Then, just behind her, she heard it—a low, throaty growl. And when she raised her head she saw, padding towards her on silent paws, a sleek black panther. As she lay helpless it came right up to her, standing over her, snarling softly, so that she felt its breath scorching her cheek, and she looked up into its blazing jade-green eyes.

But then the face seemed to shift, to become nothing more for a moment than a gold mask, then to shift again—this time into a human face. And it was human hands which, in the warm darkness, were moving over her body, stroking, caressing, drawing out of her strange responses, wild desires which flared instantly into life. She moaned and writhed on the ground beneath those roving hands, every atom of her being on fire, assailed by scarlet flames which consumed her, searing her flesh.

The figure tensed then moved its body over hers, and she turned her head frantically from side to side, her breath growing shallower and shallower, until her lungs were gasping for air. Then, as a violent shudder ran right through her, she moaned, cried out and ——

'Dany!'

There was a voice in her ear, drawing her up out of that fiery vortex into which she'd plunged. She moaned again and resisted, but the arms which were round her tightened and her eyes fluttered open. But in the near-dark all she could see was that same blurred outline, the same shadowed face, and she fought to break free.

'Dany—hush.'

This time, she leapt out of sleep, trembling violently, sweat cold on her skin, and saw, bending towards her ——

'Nick—oh, Nick!' Putting up a trembling hand to her mouth, she began to cry, huge, ragged sobs wrenching her entire frame.

'Oh, baby, don't.' He gathered her closer to him, stroking her hair, and after one last feeble effort to break free, she lay back with a sigh, letting him cradle her against his bare chest. 'Was it a nightmare?'

'Mmm,' she gulped.

'Want to tell me about it?'

'No!' Horrified, she jerked away from him again, but he gently drew her back. 'No, I was just being stupid.'

'About this goddamn forest?'

'Yes,' she lied gratefully. 'It's all a bit much for me, I think.'

'Well, don't let it get at you, honey. You're not exactly the first who's felt that way. And anyway, I've told you—we'll get out of here OK.'

She nodded, her nerves still too shredded by the erotic intensity of that dream for her to manage anything more than a faint snuffle. He raised his hand, lifting a strand of hair which clung to her wet cheek and tucking it behind her ear. His fingers rested there for a moment, then he drew them away and released her abruptly.

'Dawn's breaking, so we may as well get up.'

'Oh, must we?' she protested.

'Yes, we must.' That harsh note which she so hated was back in his voice. 'The earlier we start, the better. In case you haven't noticed, I'm at least as keen to get the hell out of this place as you are.' And, pushing back the blanket with an impatient gesture, he slid out of the shelter.

When she reluctantly crawled out to join him, then straightened up, Dany gasped. Yesterday, she'd just been too exhausted to take in their surroundings, but now she saw that their camp site was on a gentle slope beyond which the ground fell sharply away to a wide bowl of a valley, and beyond that again was another wooded ridge, a line of feathery palms marching across it. The whole scene—sky, valley, hillsides—was flooded with a wash of soft, palest apricot.

Her lips parted in a long, soundless, 'O-oh,' and she looked round at Nick, a luminous smile on her face. 'It's really beautiful,' she said huskily.

He looked down at her, his eyes holding hers, but then his mouth twisted. 'Thought this forest wasn't your scene, sweetheart. Anyway, make the most of it—I aim to get us the other side of that ridge by noon today.'

Turning away, he stooped over the pool and began fetching up handfuls of water, dashing them into his face and over his arms and shoulders—violently, as if he was trying to cleanse himself of some inner, driving demon.

Slowly, Dany went to kneel alongside him, but straight away he sprang to his feet and went over to the rucksack.

'What do you fancy for breakfast?' he asked curtly, taking out a couple of tins. 'More of that rice?'

She pulled a face. 'Ugh, no thanks.'

'Well, it'll have to be spaghetti hoops, then.'

'So you can't run to bacon and eggs—sunny-side up, of course?'

'No, I cannot. Although, if you try hard enough, those hoops might just turn into a T-bone steak—medium rare—with french fries and a side salad.' He groaned. 'Oh, God, you've got me hallucinating now.' He ran his fingers across his chin, rasping the dark stubble, then groaned again. 'Good grief—what a beard.'

With another of those quicksilver mood changes, he grinned at her, all his good humour restored—temporarily—and without warning Dany's stomach lurched, then slid slowly sideways.

'I—I've just remembered. I've got a razor in my bag.' Her voice was high and breathy. 'It's only a little one, but——'

Scrambling to her feet, she turned her back to burrow in her bag, as she fought for composure. What on earth was happening to her? First that dream—she *never* had dreams like that—and now this. But, Dany, her inner voice said agitatedly, Nick Devlin is everything you detest in a man— you know he is. Arrogant, bloody-minded, totally unpredictable, never missing a chance to put you—*you* personally— down. And yet, in that frozen moment, as he'd smiled at her, his thin lips softening, his green eyes lighting up with laughter, her insides had turned to water, so that she could barely stand.

'Is that it?'

Nick's voice came from just behind her, and glancing down she realised that she was clutching a small pink razor.

'Y-yes.' Without looking up, she handed it to him and heard his rueful laugh.

'Well, it's not quite what I'm used to, but needs must ——'

'When the Devlin drives.' An inane giggle was welling up in her, and, helpless to stop herself, she went on, 'Better the Devlin you know than the Devlin you don't know.'

As the giggle bubbled over into an almost hysterical laugh, Nick swung her round to him, tilting her face upwards. 'Are you all right?' He eyed her narrowly. 'You look flushed. You're not going down with fever on me, are you?'

'Oh, no.' But under his scrutiny she felt the heat scorch even more in her cheeks. 'I expect I got too much sun yesterday.'

'Well, I told you enough times to put your sunhat on. And how's your blister?'

'Oh, it's better now,' she said quickly.

'Let's see it.'

Reluctantly, she sat down and he began swiftly unbandaging her foot. As she looked down at his lean, tanned fingers, moving with feather-light gentleness to probe at her tender skin, the sudden thought slid into her mind: What would it be like to lie in his arms and have those fingers rove all over her flesh, drawing from her those quivering responses which she'd only ever felt in that one ecstatic dream?

Wisps from the dream brushed across her skin like cobwebs, and her breathing became rapid, her chest rising and falling. Nick glanced up sharply and, a split second too late, she dropped her lashes to screen her betraying eyes. He looked straight at her, and she knew that that cool gaze which flicked over her had taken in her moist, parted lips, the sensual hunger in her eyes. But far worse even than that—the humiliating certainty jolted through her—he knew exactly what she'd been thinking.

He said nothing, though, merely set down her foot for her to press experimentally on the ground. 'Oh, it's fine now. Thank you, Nick.'

She gave him a forced smile, but he only nodded then said brusquely, 'You'll live. I'll just renew the dressing, then while I have a quick shave you can organise the food—' he gave her a sidelong glance '—*please*. And then we'll get moving.'

CHAPTER FIVE

THE way ahead was blocked by a wide, slow-moving stream, and Nick stopped, irritably muttering something to himself. Dany let the pack slip from her back, grateful for the respite, even though it was lighter now by four days' worth of tins. Today had been just like the others—they seemed to have fallen into a pattern, with him driving them both remorselessly, covering the ground in virtual silence apart from monosyllabic grunts, loping along ahead of her, and only turning to snarl when she dropped too far behind.

Just once, when he'd stood flicking the machete against his leg and giving vent to a particularly long-suffering sigh, had she been goaded into snapping, 'We haven't all got legs half a mile long, you know.'

He'd favoured her with one look. 'Yeah, well, half-size legs for a half-size brain.'

And then he'd set off again at the same break-neck speed, leaving her, after aiming one killing look at his backbone, to stumble after him.

Now, with barely a glance at her, he hitched up his rucksack then bent to pick up hers. 'I'll take these across, then I'll have to come back and carry you.'

He made it sound as if it was the most loathsome chore imaginable. 'I can cope perfectly well on my own, thank you,' she said frostily.

He looked down at her trainers, filthy and threadbare after four days of struggling over the rough ground, and his lip curled. 'In those useless things?'

'It's not my fault. I didn't know I was letting myself in for a hundred-mile trek through the jungle—oh, *so* sorry, forest—did I?'

'If you hadn't gone out there in the first place—disobeying orders—we wouldn't be here now.'

'You're never going to let me forget that, are you?'

'Never's a long time, sweetheart—and I don't intend for you to be round me, fouling up my life, for anything like that long. But for now you can just shut up and stay right there.'

Smouldering with resentment, Dany watched as he waded out into the stream, the green, brackish water rising steadily until it was just below the top of his boots. It was perfectly all right—she'd just roll up her trousers, take off her shoes and socks and go straight in after him. Or suppose she took a running jump—after all, she'd been longing to tell him to do just that ever since they'd met, hadn't she?

At the top of the bank, just behind her, was a gnarled old cotton tree, and hanging from it were several green liana stems, thick as a man's wrist. Scrambling up, she took hold of the largest one then turned to face the stream, just as Nick, on the far bank, put down both packs and turned back. At his ferocious scowl, her heart quailed with terror, but then she beat her chest defiantly.

'Me Tarzan!'

She heard him yell, 'No, don't,' then, with a tremendous leap, she launched herself into space. Her impetus almost carried her across, and she was already bracing herself for the landing when there was a loud creak, the liana split and, helpless to save herself, she came down flat on her back in the middle of the stream. She surfaced, blinded by strands of wet hair, coughing and choking on the vile-tasting water, just as Nick reached her. Putting his hands under her arms, he dragged her to her feet.

'You little fool! Will you *ever* do what I tell you?' he demanded furiously.

'Not if I can help it.' Still defiant, she pushed her hair out of her eyes, gasping for breath.

He shook her, as if he'd been waiting a long time for that particular pleasure, then snarled, 'Well, you'd better bloody learn— from here on.' And, flinging her over his shoulder, he waded to the bank and dumped her down like a sack of turnips.

Still coughing the water out of her lungs, she stood wriggling her feet miserably in her trainers, feeling them squelch, while he faced her, hands on hips, breathing hard and regarding her coldly.

'You're going to have to get out of that lot. *Yes,*' he insisted, as she clutched at her sodden shirt. 'After all,' he added unpleasantly, 'you might just as well be out of them already.'

And looking down she realised that her clothes were clinging to her like a second skin, her trousers outlining the rounded curves of her hips and thighs, and the shirt moulding to her full, high breasts, the rosy buds of her nipples and the dusky pink areolae around them clearly visible through the all but transparent cotton.

Instinctively, she put up an arm to shield herself, but he went on brutally, 'Oh, don't fret yourself, lady—if you think shedding your clothes is a turn-on, think again.'

She winced at the vicious stab of his words, but then, gathering the shreds of her ruined dignity to her, she set her head haughtily. 'Don't you worry, either. Turning you on is the very last thing I want to do—now, or ever.'

'Well, that's a load off my mind.' She glared up at him balefully, but this time stayed silent. 'One thing's for sure, though. We can't go any further today—not now. You wait here while I go on and see if I can find a camp site with clean water—not this filthy stuff.' He jerked a thumb at the stream. 'And don't go near it. You're damn lucky I'm not picking leeches off every inch of you right now.'

When he had gone, Dany leaned up against a tree, arms folded, staring at the ground. What on earth had got into her, behaving so childishly? It was his fault— he was so bossy, so domineering that she just had to defy him, in self-defence, or be crushed totally. But no—deep inside herself she knew that wasn't the reason. She just hadn't wanted to be carried across that stream, held in his arms, her head nestled against his chest.

Not that he'd have wanted to from choice, either... If she needed any reminding of how he felt about her, he'd just made that brutally clear. In fact, ever since breaking camp that first morning, he'd seemed deliberately to have constructed a ring fence around himself, as though the very sight of her, let alone any physical contact, was distasteful to him. And he hadn't even indulged himself with any more of that sexual wordplay...

A group of gaudily plumaged birds skimmed across the surface of the stream, and a picture came to her of how, out walking one day near Gramps's house, she'd caught a fleeting glimpse of a kingfisher. How excited she'd been—yet here, in this vibrant, pulsating forest, even more brilliantly coloured birds were everywhere...

What a long time Nick was. Could he be in trouble? Could the looters have circled round ahead of them so that he'd run straight into them? The unease burgeoned instantly into full-blown panic. On the ground beside her was a branch—she snatched it up, began racing headlong through the trees, and ran straight into him, almost knocking him over. His brows came down in a thunderous scowl.

'I thought I told you——' He broke off, obviously struggling for self-control. 'Just where the hell do you think you're off to?'

She hung her head. 'I—I was worried about you. I thought those l-looters...'

Her voice trailed into nothing, and his lip curled. 'So what did you intend doing about it? Burst in to save me like a pocket-size Superman, armed to the teeth with a dead stick?'

Stung to the quick, Dany retorted hotly, 'Well, you needn't worry—I won't bother next time. I'll let them get you, and—and good riddance.'

'You do just that.'

Removing the stick from her hand, he broke it in half—just to show her what a fool she'd been, she thought sullenly—and contemptuously tossed the two bits away. He picked up his own rucksack and went to take hold of hers, but she snatched it away from him.

'I can manage it quite well, thank you.'

One shoulder lifted carelessly. 'Please yourself,' and he strode off, not even looking back to see if she was following. After about five minutes, though, he stopped, and Dany, coming up behind him, peered through a tangle of bushes then gasped.

'A *house*? A house out here?' She turned to Nick, her eyes wide.

'That's right—a *hacienda*.'

'But—is there anyone living there?'

'Take another look.'

She saw now that the lush green tide of forest had been allowed to creep right up to the building. The sloping roof was intact, though, along with the walls, still white-washed, while the wrought-iron balconies and the veranda, overhung by the purple and rose bougainvillaea and white jasmine, which loving hands had once planted and tended, remained to show that this had once been a beautiful house. Now, though, an air of gentle melancholy hung over it, and she found herself edging a little closer to Nick.

'So it's deserted?' Her voice had dropped to a whisper.

'That's right. I've been inside and had a good look round. We'll spend the night here—at least you'll have a real roof over your head, for once.'

But her mouth suddenly went dry. 'The owners—did they die?'

He glanced at her, then gave a brief laugh. 'You've been watching too many late-night movies, Ms Trent.' But then he rested an arm momentarily on her shoulders. 'Don't worry—no ghosts, I promise you.'

'But why would anyone want to live out here?'

'I seem to remember the government, some years ago, setting up a scheme to bring rubber-growing back to this area. Would-be rubber barons were enticed out from Santa Clara—given massive grants to get them started, but it didn't work out and the estates finally folded, so now the forest is taking over again. This place must be one of their *haciendas*.'

She followed him up the steps to the veranda, parting the tangled stems of sweet-scented jasmine, and on through the green-mesh door. Inside, out of the blazing sun, it was dark, with a pervading smell of damp, and she was relieved when Nick threw open a rickety shutter, letting sunlight flood in. The room was empty apart from some odds and ends of broken furniture—two plastic-covered armchairs, a bamboo chest.

The next room must have been the kitchen—there was a rough table in the centre, two straight-backed wooden chairs, units still hung on one wall, and a wood-burning stove stood near the door. Together, they went from room to room, their footsteps echoing softly, and stirring up little clouds of dust which swirled into the air. Then, at the back of the house, Nick led the way into one final room, and this time, when he pushed open the shutters, through the greenish light which filtered through the creepers Dany saw a large metal-framed bed, with a mattress still lying on it. He prodded it experimentally, and a little trail of sawdust trickled out from one of the holes.

'Well,' he said ironically, 'looks as if you'll be sleeping in five-star luxury tonight.'

'Oh, bliss.' She eyed the shabby mattress as if it were stuffed with the finest goose-down. 'But isn't it damp?'

As if on cue, she sneezed, and he said, 'There's a couple of hours' daylight yet. I'll move it out into the sun to air, while you get out of those wet things...'

Dany hitched up the blanket, which she had knotted round her, under her armpits sarong-style. Maybe she'd hang the wretched thing on the wall of her bed-sit, like a jazzy abstract painting, when she got to London—heaven knew, it had certainly become a vital feature of her life these past few days. Then, bundling up her slimy clothes, she went outside again.

Behind the *hacienda* a small stream flowed swiftly, and someone had placed flat oval boulders beside it. This must have been where the women of the house had done their washing... For a moment, she stood looking down, her throat constricted at the thought of all those shattered hopes, then, dropping to her knees, she plunged her clothes into the clear water and set to work...

'That's a good idea.'

Dany, who had just been draping her clean trousers over a low poinciana bush in the sun, swung round to see Nick dumping an armful of wood by the rear door. He sauntered across to her.

'You can wash these for me while you're at it.'

As she sat back on her heels looking up at him, he peeled off his T-shirt, which had been moulding itself damply to his torso and ribcage, and dropped it beside her. Kicking off his boots, he tossed his socks on to the T-shirt, then, before she could avert her eyes, he casually unzipped his jeans, stepped out of them, and she found herself at eye-level with those black silk briefs.

They were slung low on his narrow hips, revealing the taut horizontal muscles of his belly above, and below, the tiny black whorls of hair on his inner thighs. There was no paler band of flesh; he must sunbathe—though somehow she couldn't associate this man with indolently lounging about under a layer of suntan oil—in the nude... Beneath the satin skin of his stomach, she could see the beat of his pulse, and once again her own pulses began beating in time, as a slow clamour filled her blood.

She turned away and, seizing his clothes, threw them into the stream, then began scrubbing violently at them. When she peered again, under one arm, he was trimming the wood into logs with the machete, and whistling. Somehow, that whistling got to her in a way that not even any of his abrasive remarks had done. It showed that he was perfectly relaxed, while she — Dany forced her mind away from how she felt and grimly set to work on his shirt.

When she finally got to her feet, flexing her aching back, Nick was still slicing through the logs. Pulling up the blanket, she fetched the precious tablet of soap, which she kept wrapped in a fresh green leaf in her bag, and set off up the stream.

'Don't go far.' She thought he hadn't noticed her, but his voice pursued her.

'All right.'

She wandered up the hillside behind the *hacienda*, then saw that at one point, where the stream tumbled down in a little waterfall, someone had fixed a metal pipe to form a rough shower-head. Nick was busy back at the house, so she was quite safe. Stripping off the blanket, she stood under the cascade, soaping herself all over with slow, languid strokes, until her skin and hair were free of the taint of that sluggish stream. Then she lay in the sun to dry, stretching herself out luxuriously and idly watching half a dozen saffron-yellow butterflies flitting among the deep pink flower-heads of a hibiscus bush, until gradually her eyelids drooped . . .

'Get yourself dressed.'

The voice was harsh, and something landed heavily on her bare stomach. Dany's eyes flew open, but for a moment she could only stare dazedly up at the dark outline between her and the sun before, in a reflex action, she sat up, clutching the clothes he had thrown to her.

'I'm s-sorry.'

Her hands were trembling violently, but somehow she fumbled herself into her shirt, though it failed utterly to protect her sleek thighs from his gaze. Not that he *was* looking at her—in fact, he was looking anywhere but. A twinge of sadness, like biting on a bad tooth, brought sudden tears to her eyes. They'd come through so much together the last few days, and yet it was obvious that he loathed her as much—if not more—than ever.

'I—I must have dropped off to sleep for a minute or two.'

'An hour or two, you mean—it'll soon be dark.' And, looking round, she realised that the sun was level with the canopy of trees. 'Anyway, food's ready.' He turned away, leaving her to scramble into her panties.

'Oh, no.'

At her horrified wail, he stopped, then turned. 'What the hell's wrong *now*?'

'My ring.' She was staring down at the swirling water at her feet. 'It must have come off when I was showering.'

Her voice rose and she held up her bare left hand. With no good grace, he came back and dropped on to his stomach on the bank. As she stared down, frantically chewing on her lip and almost in tears, his hand scrabbled among the pebbles and weed for long minutes before finally coming up, clutching the ring between thumb and forefinger. Without a word, he dropped it into her outstretched palm.

'Oh, thanks, Nick,' she babbled, weak with relief. 'I—I don't know——'

'I wouldn't put it back on that finger if I were you.' His voice was remote. 'You've lost quite a bit of weight lately.'

'Yes, you're right. She squeezed the pretty garnet and pearl ring over the knuckle of her middle finger. 'It should be all right there—look.' She held it out for his inspection.

'The man's a fool!' he exclaimed suddenly—and brutally, so that she drew back as though without warning he'd struck her across the face. 'With eyes like yours, you should have a ring with a huge tawny topaz—not a pathetic thing like that.' And before she could respond he had turned on his heel and strode off.

Feeling rather subdued, Dany climbed into her trousers. What a fuss she'd made—it was no wonder Nick despised her. That, she didn't care two straws about, of course, but that he despised her ring—

how dared he? He didn't know the first thing about what she should or shouldn't wear. It was simply that Marcus didn't approve of glitzy show, and anyway, he liked her to wear neat, dainty things.

Her right hand closed protectively over the ring. Ever since that terrifying morning, she hadn't once been able to fix Marcus in her mind, and she desperately needed it now, like a pretty little talisman to link her with him. And to bring her safely back to him.

CHAPTER SIX

WHEN Dany pushed open the kitchen door, Nick was just laying out some battered cutlery and a couple of chipped bowls. He looked up, his jade eyes unsmiling.

'I found these in the unit. And these.' Striking a match, he lit half a dozen candle stumps, which were arranged down the centre of the table.

A savoury smell came from the stove, and she inhaled deeply, then rolled her eyes in ecstasy. 'A hot meal—what is it?'

'Just more of the tinned stuff, I'm afraid—vegetable soup, followed by meatballs in tomato sauce. Will that do you?'

'Wonderful. You've been really busy,' she added, with a tentative smile.

'While you've been sunning yourself.'

Still not a flicker of a smile, and Dany's eyes dropped to the table, where the candle flames glimmered on a pile of fruit.

'Mangoes!' she exclaimed. 'But where did you get them?'

'There's an old orchard a little way downstream. Most of the trees are dead, but there were a couple of mango trees left—oh, and a lime. We'll be able to have lime juice for breakfast.'

'Mm, that's marvellous.' Without thinking, she picked up one of the mangoes and breathed in its heavy scent. 'My favourite fruit.'

'So you told me,' he said drily, and Dany, remembering what he had said in reply, hurriedly set it down again, the colour in her cheeks matching the rosy flush of the fruit.

The thick spicy soup was very good, the meatballs even better. Normally, she hated meatballs—tonight, though, she devoured them greedily, and was just chasing the last fragments round the bowl when she glanced up and caught a gleam of what might almost have been laughter in Nick's sardonic eyes.

'Sorry.' She pulled a face. 'It's just that, not having had a cooked meal for nearly a week, this is food for the gods.' She couldn't resist an impish grin. 'Another of your hidden talents, Mr James.'

'A dab hand with the can-opener, you mean.'

'But you don't always live out of tins, I'm sure.'

'Well, I'm quite good at Mexican dishes—my tortillas are the talk of all the best dinner parties back in Boston.'

'Have you lived there—Mexico, I mean?'

He nodded. 'When I was a kid, my father was based in Mexico City for a while—he's an engineer—and Rosalinda, our housekeeper, used to let me mess around in the kitchen when she was in the mood.'

'And—what about your mother?' she asked delicately.

'Oh, she didn't choose to come with us.' In spite of the grown man's rigid control, some of the raw pain of the boy seeped into his voice.

'I'm sorry,' she said softly, and, barely aware of what she was doing, put her hand on his.

He looked down at it in silence for a few moments, taking in the scratches and the broken nails, then slid his own away from underneath it.

'You know something, Ms Trent?' he said roughly. 'You really are too tender-hearted for your own good. And there's no need to feel sorry. All I ever remember of a happy family life is quarrels and sil-ences—it was quite a relief all round when she finally walked out for good.' And he went back to peeling a mango, stripping away the smooth skin with long, fastidious fingers.

Finally, though, he broke the con-strained silence which had fallen between them. 'I saw some fish downstream past the orchard. Do you fancy some tomorrow?'

'For breakfast?'

He shook his head. 'No, for dinner.'

Dany, in the middle of taking a bite, gaped at him. 'Dinner! You mean we'll still be here tomorrow night?'

'I don't see why not. We've covered the ground at a good rate so far ——'

'You can say that again,' she blurted out, and his brows came down a fraction.

'And by my reckoning we're less than two days from the border.'

'Well, in that case, why don't we press on?' Her voice was tinged with panic, and he gave a rasping laugh.

'Honey, you can't be any more anxious to get there than I am. But I don't want you collapsing with exhaustion on me—I don't fancy carrying you over that border.'

'I'm quite sure you don't,' she replied acidly. 'But I've no intention of ——'

'It's even rougher terrain from now on,' he cut in smoothly. 'And you *are* exhausted. Look at the way you dropped off—just for a minute or two, of course—out there. So I've made up my mind—we'll rest up here, for tomorrow at least.'

'But suppose I want to go on?'

An infinitesimal shrug. 'There's the door.'

She stared down at the table. Never, *never* in the history of the world had there been such a cussed, domineering, hateful... She mentally added a few more epithets that would have deeply shocked Marcus, then sat, nonplussed. Nothing in her whole life had equipped her to deal with such a man. And yet the spiralling panic inside her told her that they must leave— they had to—for she had an increasingly fatalistic feeling that if they didn't reach safety soon then something terrible would happen. All the time they'd been together, there'd been an oppressiveness in the air which somehow didn't seem to come from the forest. And here at the *hacienda* it had subtly intensified, until she felt tense and on edge all the time, as though waiting for something—she wasn't sure what—to happen.

She wanted to leap to her feet, slam her fists on the table and shout, I don't care what you want—we're leaving tomorrow.

Instead, though, she put on what she hoped was her most appealing smile. 'Please, Nick, I'll be all right. I'm not at all tired now, and——'

'You can save that wide-eyed look for Medieval Marcus. Maybe it works on him, but it's wasted on me.' Deliberately, he reached across and snuffed out most of the candles. 'We'll save these for tomorrow.'

'Oh, you——' Viciously, Dany ripped the skin off another mango.

'Fancy some coffee?'

'*Coffee*?' She looked up in astonishment.

'Of course.' Now that he'd won their latest little skirmish—and when didn't he? she thought mutinously—he seemed prepared to be almost affable. 'I found a vacuum pack in the plane. Go on out to the veranda, and I'll make it.'

'No, let me.'

He gestured towards the stove. 'And when did you last operate one of these things?'

So she went outside, but then stood motionless, her hands clasped.

'Oh, Nick—come and look.'

When he stood beside her—not too near, she couldn't help noticing—she pointed. 'That sunset—did you ever see one like it in your whole life?'

Far in the west the sun was sinking. From behind bars of violet cloud leapt huge scarlet and crimson flames, tinged at their edges by molten gold from the celestial furnace. Dany swung round to him, her face alight, her hair a glowing red-gold halo, and had the strangest feeling that, though now his eyes were fixed on the horizon, a split second earlier he had been looking at her.

'Well—did you?' she repeated.

'Yes, every night for the past week.'

And with that brusque retort he went back indoors, leaving her to stand there, feeling rather foolish. Not angry, though—rather, that faint sadness again.

He had dragged the two armchairs on to the veranda, and set an up-ended packing case between them. She sat down in one of the chairs, grimacing as the plastic cover stuck to her hot back and shoulders. With the sunset, the daytime noises of the forest had faded, and the night sounds were taking over: the tree frogs had started up their ecstatic croaking, and from across the trees came the thin cry of a hunting owl.

A large emerald-green lizard appeared at the top of the steps, puffing out his crimson throat pouch; after a few minutes a smaller, paler lizard emerged from the tangled bougainvillaea, and they both darted away into the undergrowth. Lots of baby lizards soon, Dany thought with wry amusement. But really, all this teeming, pulsating lushness, wasn't it all sexual—feverish activity in the endless struggle to survive? And was this why she was so afraid of it, seeing things which she didn't wholly understand, things which were too powerful for her to control?

Nick set an old enamelled mug of coffee beside her, and she picked it up, inhaling its dark, bitter fragrance, then took a tentative sip.

'Oh, great. My first hot drink for four whole days.'

She smiled up at him, but he ignored the smile and, dropping down into the other chair, sat cradling his mug between his hands, swirling the coffee and staring moodily down at it. They were separated by inches yet he was a thousand miles away from her, and Dany sat, gazing out into the night, not daring to break that brooding silence.

Finally, though, after draining his mug, Nick uncoiled himself from his chair and disappeared into the house to emerge moments later with a tattered bundle of magazines and a small wooden box.

'I found this stuff in one of the rooms. Amuse yourself with these.'

He dropped the magazines into her lap then sat down again and opened the box, revealing to her surreptitious glance a miniature chess set. After placing the board on the packing case and setting out the pieces, he sat back, resting his chin on the bridge of his fingers and gazing down at it.

She picked up a magazine—it was in Spanish but the pictures told her it was a fashion glossy from about five years previously. By the light of the candle stub he'd placed between them, she began flicking her way through it, but over and over found her eyes being drawn back towards Nick, who was now completely engrossed in the chess, and seemingly quite oblivious to her. Instantly, he'd erected that total exclusion zone around himself, pushing her away.

He was a loner, pure and simple—he'd told her that, hadn't he? Self-sufficient, not needing any other human being—and now that he'd given her that one fleeting glimpse of his childhood before bringing the shutters down again she could begin to understand why.

The flickering candle-light was throwing his face into vivid relief against the darkness, giving his hard-planed cheek-bones an even harder edge, making the compressed line of his mouth even tauter, and giving his eyes, half-hidden by the screen of black lashes, the cold glint of green ice.

She gave up the struggle to read and leaned back in her chair, letting her gaze trace his features. How handsome he was— but he was more than just a handsome man. Even at rest, as he was now, he exuded power, an animal energy and force which was frightening in its raw potency.

Her mouth was dry, her palms clammy, and once again she felt deep inside her a sense of expectation, of something—she didn't know what—waiting to happen. But then, as a faint roll of thunder rumbled far away, and the sheen of lightning briefly lit the far horizon, she drew back even further into her chair and, snatching up another magazine, began turning the pages with clumsy fingers.

This one seemed to be an international gossip rag: movie stars by their azure swimming-pools, the young of minor European royalty, and presumably the current scandals in their love-lives, although as the text was again in Spanish it was all unintelligible to her. She went on flicking through it, but then stopped dead. There, staring out at her, was surely—yes, there was his name—Nick Devlin. He looked so different, though, dressed for some jet-set gala in white dinner-jacket and black tie, and his arm rested round the slender waist of a glossy blonde in a maximum-cleavage black dress. He was turning to smile at her, and Dany felt behind that sleek panther-like smile a sexual magnetism which all but leapt off the flimsy paper.

Nick had never smiled—never would smile at her like that... She stared down at the faded photograph, from one face to the other, unpleasant sensations churning over in her stomach until a strangled sound, almost a whimper, was wrenched from her.

He glanced up and must have seen her face. 'What's the matter?'

'Nothing.' But a tight pain had settled round her ribs like a vice.

Quite unable to look at him, she clutched at the magazine but, reaching over, he neatly twitched it from her fingers, and she saw his eyes skim the double page then stop. He smiled to himself, and Dany, alert to every movement, could have leapt at him, claws bared, and raked that little secret smile off his face.

Then, 'Good grief—Annabel. Yes——' he held the picture closer to the candle-flame '—I'm sure it's her. Or is it Sarah-Jane?'

'Yes, it must be difficult for you to re-member,' Dany snapped. 'Just one of thousands, no doubt.'

'Well, not quite.' His white panther-like teeth showed in a grin, then he tossed the magazine across to her again, but she closed it deliberately and dropped it on to the pile. 'Do I detect just the faintest note of censure, Ms Trent?'

'Of course not.' She tossed back her hair, taking refuge from the pain in angry attack.

'What you choose to do with your life has absolutely nothing to do with me.'

'Precisely,' he agreed coolly. 'But, for your information, yes, it's true; I've known a lot of women. It's also true that I've cared deeply for some of them, wanted to please all of them and leave them happy. But —— ' the green eyes were subjecting her to a challenging stare '—*leave* is the operative word. I've never met a woman yet for whom, once the passion had cooled, I'd be prepared to give up my freedom.'

'I see.' To bring an end to this barbed conversation, Dany reached down for another magazine, but he continued,

'Does it offend your delicate sensibilities to be in such close contact with an untrammelled male, Ms Trent?'

'Certainly not,' she said with icy hauteur, and, leaning back, crossed her legs and opened the first page.

'Good. Because I wouldn't like to do that, Ms Trent.' And from under her lashes she saw him return to his chess game, instantly absorbing himself in it once more.

Dany abandoned the magazine and sat, chin in hand, watching him, as the pieces on the board tacked to and fro in some silent stylised battle.

'Why did you move that one?' she asked suddenly.

'To protect my back.'

He did not look up, and gradually she edged further and further forward until finally she slid to her knees and sat, both elbows resting on the packing case. He moved another piece then glanced up sharply, and she saw herself reflected in the candle-glow in his eyes.

'If you want to play, just tell me.'

He didn't sound angry, just exasperated, but she drew back instantly. 'Oh, no—I can't play chess.'

'No, well, that figures. After all, it's a game which requires a high degree of logic—and a strictly disciplined mind.'

'I see.' Her mouth drooped, and with a heart-felt sigh he cleared the board with one sweep of his hand.

'OK, OK, I'll give you a lesson....'

* * *

'*No*. Remember what I said—you can never move a pawn backwards.'

'Sorry.' Dany quickly removed the tiny pawn and set it down hesitantly on another square.

'Yes, that's it.' He moved one of his pieces. 'Now, what are you going to do about my bishop?'

'Well,' she hedged. 'How about this?' And picking up her queen, she set it down alongside Nick's piece.

'Well done.'

He smiled at her in genuine pleasure, and all at once she thought, Soon, I shall never see him again, but I shall always remember this moment. The flickering candle-light, those fireflies out there in the warm darkness, the sweet smell of jasmine above our heads, and Nick smiling at me. The bitter-sweet pain shot through her, and she moved her hand convulsively across the board.

'No, my move.'

Nick stretched out his hand at the same instant, and their fingertips met. It was just for a split second then they both jerked back as though the other hand had stung theirs, staring at each other, lips parted. She felt that strange tension hiss softly in the air between them, that sleeping serpent rousing again, then Nick said brusquely, 'You're tired. Bed for you.'

'Oh, no, the game's not over,' she protested, but feebly, as though still held in the clutches of that out-of-time moment.

Nick gave her a crooked grin. 'Yes, it is.' And with one fluid movement he simultaneously captured her last remaining pawn and imprisoned her king. 'Checkmate, I think.'

He stood up, and before she could shrink back into her chair had scooped her up into his arms. Bending, he picked up the candle stub and put it into her hand, then carried her indoors and into the kitchen, shouldering open the door.

Desperately, Dany tried to rivet every atom of her attention to that guttering candle-flame, yet with every grain of her being she was aware of his strong arms wrapped around her, his chest wall against her breast, separated only by thin cotton.

In the bedroom, he let her drop on to the edge of the bed. Prising the candle from her clutching fingers, he set it down on the bare floorboards and stood looking down at her, an unreadable expression on his shuttered face.

'Into bed.'

'All right—I'll just take my trainers off.'

Hitching up one foot, she began fiddling with the fragile laces, but the grey fatigue which was now stealing through her made her fingers stiff and clumsy. She felt him watching her for a moment then he went down on his haunches and, pushing her hands firmly out of the way, undid first one shoe then the other and set them down beside the bed.

He waited as she lay down on the mattress, curling herself under the rough blanket, then, stooping down, snuffed out the candle. She felt his hand rest lightly on her forehead for an instant, then he said quietly, 'Goodnight, Dany—sleep well.'

'But where are *you* going?' As his foot-steps receded across the room, she raised herself on one elbow. 'Aren't you sleeping here?'

There was a silence, then, 'No, I don't think so. I'll pull the two chairs together.'

'But you can't sleep on them,' she protested in agitation. 'You—you won't be comfortable.'

'Sweetie, I'm so tired I'd sleep on a tightrope slung across Niagara.' His voice was wry.

'But I—I want you to sleep here—with me.'

'No—not tonight.' Her senses, sharpened by the darkness, caught the faint underthread of tension in his voice.

'Why not?' she demanded. 'We've slept together for the last four nights, haven't we?'

Another pause. 'Yes, but that was different.'

'I don't see why. After all, the way we both feel about each other——' Her voice trembled into silence, then she went on softly, 'Please, Nick—stay with me.'

'Why—you're not scared, are you?'

'Yes—yes, I am.' Gratefully, she snatched at the excuse. 'That story you told me—about the snake that came into your tent when you were——'

'God, I wish I'd never mentioned that bloody bushmaster,' he broke in angrily. 'I've told you a hundred times, for every venomous snake out there there are dozens of harmless ones. And anyway, while I was making the coffee I came in here to check. No wildlife—except a few roaches, and I saw all of them off.'

'Yes, but...' she was improvising, not at all sure why she so much wanted Nick to remain with her, knowing only that she desperately needed him here '...didn't you hear that rustling noise just then? I'm sure there's something out there.'

'No, I did not hear anything. And in any case, any snake will be even less keen to meet you than you are to meet him.'

'I doubt that.'

Dany gave a small laugh, but it changed halfway to a husky little croak. Nick came back beside the bed and took hold of her hands, so that she could feel his callused palms, his thumb gently stroking the back of her right hand. He was doing it to soothe her, she knew; and yet that soft, rhythmic back and forth was hypnotising her, sending peculiar messages pinging from her fingers to her wrist and up into her arm, until her eyes half closed and she swayed towards him, so that a sliver of moonlight coming through a tiny gap in one of the shutters cast a pale gleam on her face.

'You know something?' His voice sounded almost tender. 'You look about twelve years old sometimes.'

'And I sometimes behave like it too,' she whispered mournfully.

A wry laugh. 'Well, I wasn't going to say it. But you wouldn't be Dany Trent without the occasional lapse, would you?' Another slight pause. 'OK, you win—I'll stay. I'll close the shutters, though, just to keep any stray bushmasters in their place.'

He released her hand, there were soft creaks from the boards then the shutters were banged to. Returning unerringly to the far side of the bed—like those jade-eyed jaguars prowling outside, he could obviously see in the dark—then the mattress dipped slightly as he sat down. She heard the faint sounds as he unzipped his boots and kicked them off, then he slid in beside her.

'Still frightened?' he whispered.

In the darkness, Dany gave a sleepy smile. 'No.'

'That's good.' And, turning over on his side, well away from her, he seemed to drop into instant sleep.

For Dany, though, worn out as she was, sleep simply refused to come. Maybe she was overtired—or maybe it was that, after all, Nick was right. It *was* different from the last few nights, when they had camped under a rough roof of palm branches. Tonight, as he had known, in the shared intimacy of a real bed, even on this lumpy, sawdust-leaking mattress, it was as if they

were lovers, or even—she clutched the unnerving thought to her then thrust it away
again—married . . .

Some time in the night, a whining mos-
quito disturbed her. She lay, eyes open wide
to the silent darkness, then realised, first
that she now lay not rigidly on the edge of
the bed, but in the middle, and second, that
she was snuggled into Nick's body, his
warm, even breath on her nape, the belt of
his jeans rubbing softly against her lower
back—and finally that his arm lay across
her, as though holding her to him.

Appalled, she tensed in every muscle and
began to inch away from him, a hair's
breath at a time. She had almost slid from
under that heavy arm when Nick muttered
something in his sleep and the arm tightened possessively over her.

She mustn't wake him—he was obviously so exhausted. Dany gave in and
rolled gingerly back to her former position
until the arm, as if sensing her surrender,
relaxed. He must, in sleep, have thought

she was one of his girlfriends—Annabel, or Sarah-Jane, or his latest, maybe. She gave a rueful little smile, but then the sudden stab of pain wrenching through her made her draw in her breath in a soundless whimper. It was a long time before she drifted back off to sleep...

When she finally woke, bands of sunlight were filtering through cracks in the shutters, and Nick had gone. She slid her hand across to his half of the bed, but the mattress was cold and only a faint sag indicated where he had slept. She yawned and sat up, stretching every limb, then, sliding out from under the scratchy blanket, she padded out into the kitchen.

He wasn't there, either. One of the chipped mugs stood on the table, filled with lime juice and water, together with the rest of the mangoes and a tin of baked beans. She drank every drop of the lime, quite certain that she'd never tasted anything so good, then peeled and ate a mango. The beans she simply couldn't face—one of the good things about the tropics at a time like this was that you often didn't feel like solid food, she decided, wrinkling her nose at the tin.

Taking another mango, she went to stand at the top of the veranda steps. The sun was high in the sky—almost overhead. She must have slept for hours; no wonder Nick had given up waiting for her. But where was he? All the time she ate the mango she listened for him, but he didn't come so she threw away the stone, fetched her trainers and the soap—now a thin shadow of itself—and went off to her shower.

She deliberately took a long time, standing under the cold cascade of water until her flesh was chill, expecting him to have returned by the time she got back to the *hacienda*, but there was still no sign of him—except a fresh pile of fruit on the table. So he had been back—and gone again. He'd probably looked in to the bedroom and knew that she was up, but he hadn't waited to see her.

Her mind scarcely on what she was doing, Dany took one of the mangoes and rubbed it gently against her soft cheek, a little frown puckering her arched brows, before finally laying it down with the others again. She found a cracked dish and very carefully arranged all the fruit on a bed of jasmine leaves to form a scented glossy pyramid.

She wandered back out on to the veranda, and stood idly pulling off scarlet bougainvillaea heads and aiming them at the machete, which stood propped up by the steps, all the time listening for foot-steps. But at last the game bored her, and to try to quell that strange restlessness which had taken hold of her she went back indoors, drifting aimlessly from room to room until she once more reached the bedroom.

Taking hold of the shutters, she pulled them fully open to let in the air, then, as she turned back, noticed in a corner recess a narrow door. A built-in wardrobe, perhaps. But when, rather nervously, she tugged it open, she saw a small closet, empty apart from a wooden chest.

It was a struggle to open it, but when at last she eased back the rusting hinges she saw layers of crumpled tissue paper, and when she tentatively pushed them open with one finger she saw a flowered fabric. Slightly breathlessly, she drew it out and, holding it up, saw that it was a simple cotton summer dress, faded along the creases. Dany held it up against her—she and this unknown woman must be much the same size.

Under it were other clothes, mainly dresses, but one man's beige linen suit, and some children's T-shirts and shorts. Tears pricked her eyes as she gazed at the shirts, with their faded cartoon pictures and slogans—this family, coming out here with such high hopes, then being driven back by the unrelenting forest...

At the very bottom of the chest was a separate package, wrapped in cloth. As she opened it, a faint spicy smell drifted to her, and when she shook out the dress inside she let out her breath in a long, awed, 'O-o-h.'

It was an evening dress of pale amber silk, its low-cut neckline edged with ruffles of heavy cream lace, more lace edging the full-length skirt. Surely, it must have been a family heirloom—certainly, it was the most beautiful dress Dany had ever seen. Without warning, a tight fist closed round her throat. The other dresses, yes—but how could any woman have borne to leave this behind? Nick must be right—they'd been so disheartened when their dreams turned to ashes that it had been too much trouble even to gather up this wonderful gown.

Carefully folding it up again, she replaced it in the chest, along with the other clothes, then wandered back out to the veranda. From habit, she glanced at her wrist, but there was only the pale mark where her watch had been; the fine metal bracelet had been ripped off, unnoticed, in a struggle through some dense undergrowth a couple of days before.

But it must be well into the afternoon by now. Surely, *surely* he'd come back soon. And if he didn't, well, she certainly wasn't going to search for him again and risk having her head snapped right off this time. On the other hand, though, her pride wouldn't allow her to moon around here any longer till he graciously chose to come back. She'd—yes, she'd go and find that orchard, pick some limes for tomorrow's breakfast.

She made her way along the stream, pausing just once to sniff at the sweet perfume of a hibiscus flower, until she came to what must have been the orchard—very overgrown but still with a few fruiting trees. She found the lime, its gnarled branches loaded down with the small, bitter green fruits, and, pulling out her shirt from her waistband, she made a bowl of it, to hold a dozen of them.

Just beyond the orchard she could hear the faint splash and tumble of a little waterfall. Maybe she'd sit by it and cool her sticky feet. Leaving the limes in a little heap, she pushed her way through the barrier of waist-high ferns, then stopped dead. Ahead, the stream flowed gently over some mossy stones, then ran into a deeper, slow-moving pool, and lying on his stomach, stripped to the waist, his dark head propped on one hand, the other trailing through the water, was Nick.

CHAPTER SEVEN

DANY was sure she hadn't made a sound, and yet, as though some extra sense had warned him, Nick turned sharply. He frowned, and for a split second she saw impatience, even anger in his face, but as she made an involuntary movement to turn and go he gestured her peremptorily towards him.

'So you've tracked me down at last,' he grunted. 'I wondered how long it would take you.'

Oh, Nick, I've missed you so much. Why have you kept away from me all day? The words trembled on her tongue, but instead she jutted her small, rounded chin and retorted, 'Don't flatter yourself—I wasn't looking for you. I found the orchard, and was just on my way back when I heard the waterfall. But don't worry, I'll go now and leave you in peace.'

'No. Now you're here, you may as well stay.' Easing himself on to his haunches, he looked up at her, his eyes narrowed against the sun. 'You look better.'

'I feel better.' She smiled almost naturally at him. 'You were right—I was exhausted, but I'm fine now.'

'Hmm.' He pursed his lips. 'But maybe you need an extra night's sleep—plus half the day again, of course—before we tackle that final section. We'll stay here one more day.' And, throwing himself down on to his stomach again, he began staring fixedly into the water once more.

Another day at the *hacienda*. Of course, if it was anything like today, she'd see next to nothing of him, so that would be all right... But another evening, sitting out on the veranda with him, the scent of jasmine making her senses reel as though she'd drunk champagne... And another night alongside him in that bed, maybe even curled up again beside that wonderful body, the tapered waist, the superbly muscled back and shoulders, as smooth and glossy as the pelt of a forest cat ——

Dragging her eyes from him, she began jerkily twisting her engagement ring round and round on her finger. She barely felt it, though, as, very slowly, fear began to spiral inside her. She ought to be desolate at the thought of spending yet another day here— ought to have assured him she was quite well enough to go on—insisted on going on. Ought, yes, when every step would bring her nearer Marcus... But every one of those same steps would also take her further from Nick.

'Well, are you going to help or aren't you?'

Withdrawing his hand from the water, he gave her ankle a swift tug which brought her down to her knees on the bank beside him.

'Help you? What are you doing?'

'Catching your supper.'

He jerked a thumb, and for the first time she saw, lying in the lush grass, several small silvery fish. She looked round, puzzled.

'What with?' He was so capable that it would have been child's play, no doubt, for him to construct a superb rod and line, but there was nothing.

'This.' He held up his right hand. 'Haven't you ever tickled fish?'

'Certainly not.'

'Amazing. And I thought it was an essential part of the education of every pocket-sized Superman.'

Her lips tightened. 'Not in my case, it wasn't.'

'Well, it's not easy.'

'Why? No, don't tell me,' she went on belligerently, 'it demands a high degree of logic and a strictly disciplined mind.'

'Not exactly.' His white teeth gleamed. 'More absolute stillness and patience, which, for a hyper-active brat like you, would be quite a——' He broke off. 'You've got pollen on your nose.'

'What?' His mercurial changes of mood were leaving her dizzy.

'Pollen. You've been sniffing flowers.' Reaching out, he tilted her face to his so that their eyes were centimetres apart, then murmured, almost as if to himself, 'It's like golden freckles. Keep still.'

Very gently, he brushed his fingertip across the end of her nose, pursed his lips to blow the pollen away in a little cloud, then let his fingers rest momentarily on the side of her face.

But as she stared at him, mesmerised, he removed it and went on briskly, 'Now, this is what you do. Get down on your stomach and very slowly slide your hand into the water—like this; keep your fingers apart, letting them go with the current. And watch until a fish swims in—then grab him. That's all there is to it.'

'All?'

'Yes. Oh, and in case you're wondering——' another slanted smile '—you don't *have* to take your shirt off for this particular sport. That's optional—rolling your sleeves up will do nearly as well.'

For the next hour or more they lay side by side, their hands drifting like weed in the clear water. Once, their fingertips touched, and Dany drew back sharply, as though from an electric shock, muttered a 'Sorry' and took good care that it didn't happen again.

Nick had caught two more small fish, but somehow they always eluded her. Try as she might, she could not properly give her mind to the fishing when every fibre of her was prickling with the awareness of that gleaming, utterly masculine torso stretched out alongside her. He, of course, she thought resentfully, had no such problem; as usual, he was completely wrapped up in what he was doing, frowning slightly, his eyes shadowed by the hooded lids, his mouth taut with concentration. And yet, in spite of the tightness, the hard-edged lines of his face, which gave him an almost monk-like austereness, there was a sensuality lurking in the thin lips which she'd never noticed before.

He looked up, caught her gaze, and something flickered in his eyes—a swift green fire. For an endless split second of time their glance held, that hissing tension wreathing itself around them both once again, but then he exclaimed, 'Look out— you've got one!'

Closing her hands instinctively, Dany brought up a wriggling silver body, and Nick cried exultantly, 'It's a big one—give it me.'

But, as he leaned towards her, quite deliberately she opened her hand, the fish arched on her palm, fell to the water and with a flick of silver was gone.

'What the hell did you do that for? It was a beauty.' Nick was staring at her in astonishment, and she hung her head.

'I—I don't know. I suppose it was so alive, I just didn't want you to kill it.'

He expelled a long breath. 'Oh, so it's just more of your very own brand of logic, then. You won't object to eating those, I presume?' He gestured towards the fish he had caught, then scowled fiercely at her again.

Snatching at the chain around her neck, she thrust the gold jaguar mask towards him.

'See this? You look just like this when you're angry—do you know that? All snarling lips and flashing eyes.'

'Be warned, then, honey.' He was still breathing heavily. 'Jaguars gobble up mini-Tarzans like you before breakfast.'

'I am *not* a mini-Tarzan,' she snapped indignantly.

'No?' His eyes ranged over her hair, tightly drawn up into a knot at her nape, her shapeless drill shirt and trousers, and his lip curled. 'Well, you've got me fooled, then, sweetheart—you're certainly no Jane, either.'

As she winced at the careless gibe, he sprang to his feet and, pulling a green bamboo stem from a nearby clump, threaded it neatly through the fish. Without even looking to see if she was following, he snatched up his shirt and set off back towards the *hacienda*.

He met her on the veranda and said brusquely, 'The fish are in the kitchen— I'll see to them later, after I've had a shower.' And, clattering down the steps, he strode away.

He couldn't bear to be in her company, he detested her so much. Dany had been standing, watching him go; now his figure blurred suddenly, and with the back of her hand she dashed the brimming tears from her eyes. In that case, why, oh, why was he prolonging the agony for both of them? Tonight, she'd tell him once and for all that she was fit enough to get over that ground—if necessary, crawling on hands and knees, she told herself fiercely, just so long as she got away from Nick Devlin soon—and for good.

She went on heavily into the kitchen, dragging each foot as though it were set in concrete. The fish lay beside the stove. She wouldn't touch them, of course—it was more than her life was worth, and anyway she didn't want to, but she could at least set the table. Listlessly, she tipped out the limes she had carried back with her, then piled up the mangoes and arranged the candles down the centre of the rough table. It still looked very bare, though, so on an impulse she went back to the veranda, snapped off some bougainvillaea heads and laid them between the candles.

And all the time her ears were strained, hoping to hear Nick coming back. What a fool you are, she told herself scornfully. Of course, it was only because she didn't like being alone out here in the forest, but even so there were worse things than lone-liness—a silent, morose companion, locked in his own thoughts, for one. If he didn't choose to come back till midnight, well, she didn't care *that* much. And, tearing the last lacy bougainvillaea head in two, she laid the two halves down very precisely in the centre of the table.

The sun was low when at last she heard him. She was perched on one of the arm-chairs out on the veranda, and he came up the steps slowly, without seeing her at first. When he did catch sight of her, sitting like a statue, he stopped.

'Hi.' He spoke not quite to her, more to the air beside her.

'Hi,' she responded carefully, determined that the new Dany would not expose herself to any more of his taunts.

'I'll see to the fish. Fancy a twist of lime with them?'

'That would be lovely,' she said politely, and got to her feet. 'I'll go and get ready, then.'

She closed the bedroom door and leaned up against it, feeling sheer misery, black as the night which would soon fall around them, ooze through every part of her. Why did he hate her so much? And was the world full of men like him: unnerving, unsettling, dangerous to be with? If so, then the sooner she got back to Marcus the better. These days, though, even the calming thought of Marcus gave her no sense of security—that dreadful dream seemed to have done something permanent to her mind, so that she was still quite unable to draw her to him or put a face to the shadowy outline which was him.

Slowly straightening up, she went over to the wide windowsill, where she kept her bag and, fishing out her mirror, peered into it. Her eyes were wide and over-bright, her mouth tremulous and, beneath the light tan, her face was pale. To look at her, one more cutting word from him and she'd crumple at his feet in tears.

Well, she wasn't going to. Snatching up her lip-gloss, she swiftly outlined her full mouth, rubbing her lips together and finally blotting them on a piece of torn tissue. Her heavy hair, which out here she kept caged up with pins, for coolness, was a mess, half up, half wisping round her face. She tucked the loose strands in behind her ears, then glanced down at herself, flicking a couple of tiny dead leaves from her trousers, and pulled a face. Lucky she wasn't dining at the Ritz...

Nick would be in evening dress, like in that faded photograph—maybe a frilly white shirt, or a beautifully embroidered silk one. While she—what would she be wearing? Perhaps that little black satin dress which she'd bought back in the January sales but hadn't yet had the courage to parade in for Marcus. Perhaps something new, bought specially. Or maybe—her stomach gave a jolt, half apprehensive, half excited, and her eyes flew to the closet door. He'd think she was mad—if he even noticed, that was. She was beginning to think he wouldn't register if she grew three heads.

Pocket-sized Superman . . . mini-Tarzan . . . you're certainly no Jane, either. . . I like my women to be just that— all-woman . . .

Of course, she didn't even know if it fitted her, did she? Next moment, Dany was beside the chest, ripping aside the tissue paper and pulling out the dress. With trembling hands, she pulled off her trousers, then, too impatient to undo the buttons, dragged her shirt over her head and caught up the dress.

It drifted down her body like cool water; she smoothed the skirts and settled her breasts into the low-cut bodice, then struggled with the tiny buttons. It was a fraction tight—a week ago she'd never have squeezed into it, she thought ruefully. But surely that was all to the good—once and for all, she'd show that *swine*.

There was no mirror, of course, but she peered down at herself. Her slender waist and flat stomach were enhanced by the folds of amber silk, the rich curves of her breasts, thrusting against the pin-tucked bodice, were shadowed by the sweep of pale lace, her neck and shoulders bare, as though rising from creamy foam.

Just one more thing was needed. Yanking the pins out of her hair, she shook it out, letting it cascade like red-gold fire to her shoulders, smoothed it down, then, head high, even though her heart was pounding against her ribs, she marched back to the kitchen.

Nick did not see her at first. He was at the stove, his back to her, and he could never have heard her above the sizzling fish. But as she stood frozen in the doorway, her skirts rustling softly, he stiffened, as if sensing her behind him, then slowly turned.

In the pale candle-light, she saw the jade eyes widen slightly as his gaze went to her hair, then down over her neck and shoulders, taking in the luscious fullness of her breasts, their soft, hurried rise and fall against the silk. And at his expression Dany, terrified suddenly, realised for the first time exactly what she'd done, and had to beat down the almost overwhelming desire to flee back to the bedroom, rip off this lovely dress and replace it with her old—safe—shirt and trousers.

'Where the hell did you get that?' He spoke at last, but there was a faint thread of tension in his voice.

'In a chest—in the bedroom.' Her own voice was tight, as she fought for composure. 'Th—there are other things there— a man's suit, but I don't think it would fit you.'

'I—didn't realise we were dressing for dinner.'

His eyes were holding hers, but somehow she forced her gaze to slide past him, and she saw, standing in the middle of the table, a bottle of white wine.

She gasped. 'Where did you find that?'

'Oh, you're not the only one to have done some exploring.' The tone was nearly back to normal. 'There's a cellar of sorts down below. It's almost empty, apart from a load of empties—oh, and quite a few spiders.' Dany gave a shudder. 'But I found a couple of these.'

As though grateful for movement, he jerked open his penknife, revealing a tiny corkscrew, and inserted it into the cork. 'I don't know what it's like, of course, and it can't exactly be served chilled, but I'll be thankful for any change from that vile rum.'

The cork came out cleanly, and after pouring some wine into one of the mugs he sipped it cautiously. 'Hmm. Plonk—but drinkable.' He filled up his mug, then hers. 'The fish should be ready, so——'

He gestured to the table, but when she still stood, her legs utterly refusing to move, he came up to her, his face enigmatic, and bowed slightly. Raising her fingers to his lips, he kissed the back of her hand—the merest hummingbird's wing of a kiss—then said, with the slightest hint of irony, 'Dinner is served, *mademoiselle*.'

His own composure allowed her to recover hers—on the surface, at least. 'Thank you.' She swept him a deep curtsy, then, as he pulled back her chair, she sank down into it gratefully, her legs still trembling under her.

As soon as he turned back to the stove, she took a gulp of wine. Well, as he'd said, it was an improvement on that fire-water—just. She drank another large mouthful as he slid her plate across, with several crisply grilled fish, and some limes, neatly sliced.

'Thanks.' She actually managed a real smile this time. 'It looks delicious.'

He grimaced. 'Rather too-too for me. Nouvelle cuisine, I mean. I don't usually go for it, I'm afraid—I prefer my plate to look slightly less like a still-life by Braque.'

'Yes, I know what you mean.' Dany gratefully seized at this chance to move on to neutral ground. 'A sliver of pâté you can see through, two fingers of toast —— '

'And a couple of radishes heavily disguised as rosebuds. Exactly.' He rolled his eyes in disgust, then pointed with his fork to her plate. 'Anyway, what there is of it— eat up...'

'More wine?' Nick held up the bottle.

'Oh, no, thanks. I've had plenty.' In fact, as well as the mugful, he had halved two large mangoes and poured generous helpings of wine into each. 'I don't usually drink.'

'Not at all?'

'Well, no—I don't really like it.' She bit her lip, half embarrassed at her own failings. 'I suppose you do. I mean —— '

She broke off as he laughed, the first natural laugh she'd heard from him all day.

'I'm not a wino, if that's what you mean. But yes, I do like wine, in its place. And you don't only because you haven't been properly taught.' There was a jagged edge to his voice for a moment, and she looked away quickly. 'Haven't you ever had champagne?'

'Well, once or twice, at weddings—oh, and Gramps's sixtieth birthday. But apart from that, no,' she admitted reluctantly. 'Well, go on, say it—I'm a bit of a freak. On top of being a mini-Tarzan, that is.'

'I promise you, Dany ——' his voice was suddenly husky '—after this evening, I shall never again make the mistake of accusing you of being a Johnny Weismuller look-alike.' His eyes drifted over her as she sat motionless, and she was conscious again of the tightening of her skin, the quickening of her breath. 'You look absolutely gorgeous.'

His gaze was fixed now on the tiny pulse at the base of her throat, and there was silence for a long moment, while she almost thought she could hear her heart pounding. Then she realised that in fact it was another of those distant rolls of thunder.

'W-will there be a storm, do you think?' Perhaps this explained why this heavy, charged atmosphere still hung oppressively around them, as if waiting for the tension—somehow—to be broken.

'Could be. The rainy season isn't too far off now.'

He poured more wine into his mug but sat without touching it, flicking his spoon against his plate instead. His eyes were lowered now and she could risk looking across at him, the unruly hair flopped forward over his brow, the hard lines of his jaw softened by candle-light and dark stubble.

He seemed to catch her thought, though, for glancing up, he smiled ruefully, rasping his hand over his chin. 'Sorry about the beard. That razor of yours doesn't seem quite man enough for the struggle.'

She smiled back. 'You look very handsome, Nick.'

It was out before she could snatch it back, and she gave a little gasp. Heavens, the wine—she really shouldn't have drunk so much. 'I tell you what,' she went on, struggling for normality, 'when we get out of this, I'll buy you a bottle of champagne.'

'No.' He gave her a soft smile, which for some strange reason made her want to put her head down on the table and weep. 'I'll buy *you* a bottle. No, a whole case—just to begin your wine education, of course. Bollinger '79, I should think. Or maybe a sweet white wine. Yes, an '89 Sauternes— that's the wine for you. Lush and sweet and honeyed, and,' his voice dropped slightly, 'scented with the promise of all the flowers of summer.'

'My goodness.' Nick's sensuous words all but had her mind reeling. Now she gave a rather high, breathless laugh. 'You make it sound more like a magic spell than a wine.'

'Oh, it is, Dany,' he said gravely, 'and magic things can happen after you've drunk it.'

'Well——' she smiled uncertainly, not quite sure how much he was serious and how much he was gently mocking her '——shall we have coffee now?'

Nick drained his wine then stood up. 'I'll make it—you go outside.'

Picking up one of the candles, she took it out on to the veranda, then sat, chin on hand, gazing down into the tiny flickering flame. There was only an inch or so of candle left, just enough for one more evening, and then—darkness. There was a tight feeling around her chest, and to ease it she inhaled deeply, feeling the jasmine perfume fill her.

But then, as another rumble of thunder sounded—louder this time—something large and white and shapeless came fluttering on to the veranda above her head, and with a piercing shriek she leapt to her feet. Next moment, Nick, the machete in his hand, appeared.

'Dany! What on earth —— ?'

She took away one of the hands she was holding to her mouth and pointed. 'There!'

He followed her gaze then let out his breath in a release of tension and exasperation. 'Oh, God—what you do to me. I thought you'd got a marauding jaguar out here, at the very least.'

As if to give vent to his feelings, he hurled the machete into the wooden floor, where it held and stayed upright, vibrating softly, before going over to where the intruder hung, quivering, on one of the shutters.

When Dany edged away, backing up against the tangle of jasmine and bougain-villaea, he said sharply, 'Stand still. If you frighten it, it'll probably hurl itself into the candle-flame.'

Very gently, he raised both hands and captured the creature between them, but as he came towards her she shrank away.

'No. Don't be scared.' Opening his hands a fraction, Nick looked down, then exclaimed, 'Good grief, it's a moon moth!'

He glanced up at her. 'It's like you—way off its home patch. The eastern seaboard of the States is more its territory.'

'Oh, poor thing.' Dany's heart swelled; another helpless creature, completely out of its natural element here in this forest. 'Will it die, do you think?'

'Who knows? Maybe—maybe not. But come and look.'

He parted his fingers slightly again, and as she steeled herself to gaze at the huge insect it fluttered its wings beseechingly. She looked at the strong hands holding it as delicately as any woman would, and felt her heart twist painfully. This was a side of Nick she'd never seen till now; she knew the arrogance, the toughness, but here was something else altogether—the tenderness, as of a lover.

'Isn't she beautiful?' he whispered.

'Yes—yes, she is,' she replied breathlessly. The moth's wings were a pale creamy white, tinged along the veins with softest green, and its long, sweeping tail was brushing against Nick's wrists.

'Touch it.'

Obediently, she softly stroked its head. 'Oh, Nick, it's like velvet.'

She looked up and saw his eyes fixed on her lips as she spoke, and drew back her hand sharply. He walked down the veranda steps, well away from the candle, and she saw him open his hands. There was a soft rustle, a blur of white, and then he was coming back. He stood looking down at her as she, quite unable to meet his eyes, fidgeted with her skirt, pleating and un-pleating the silk.

'You've got some flower petals caught in your hair. Keep still.'

She felt his hands parting the strands of hair then sliding round to cup her chin, tilting her face so that she was forced to meet his gaze.

'Dany?' he said huskily, and when she smiled tremulously at him he took her hand, raising it to his lips again. This time, though, instead of releasing it, he turned it over and, keeping his eyes fixed on her, began kissing the palm, brushing his lips across her moist skin in slow, sensuous movements that sent intense sensations jolting up her arm and to every furthest corner of her trembling body.

When his mouth left her palm, to start trailing down each finger in turn, she closed her eyes, swaying on her feet. And when finally he moved from the thumb back to the soft pad at its base to drop sliding, nipping kiss-bites across it, she sank her teeth into her soft inner mouth in a vain attempt to hold back the whimpers of pleasure-pain he was drawing from her.

CHAPTER EIGHT

WHEN at last Nick stopped Dany opened her eyes, dazed by sensation, almost unable to breathe. He was looking down at her, his eyes dark.

'Dany?' he repeated.

When she did not reply, only smiled softly at him, he put his hands on her shoulders and very slowly drew her into his arms. Then, as she stopped breathing altogether, his head came down, his lips covered hers, warm and alive and blotting out everything except the taste and feel of his mouth against hers: sweet yet slightly salt, and with a faint taste of wine.

His lips brushed softly to and fro, exactly as he had done with her palm—and with the same devastating effect. Then, with the very tip of his tongue, he outlined the edge of her mouth, first the top then the bottom, in a caress so erotic that she clutched at him, her fingers raking across his back and fastening on handfuls of shirt.

Sliding one hand down from her shoulders to the small of her back, he rested it there, fingers splayed against the tops of her buttocks, and moulded her into himself so that she felt his body's urgent, raw need of her. As his tongue probed the inner recesses of her mouth, plundering the sweetness, his other hand moved down the line of her bare shoulder and came to rest against one of her breasts. He cupped its fullness in his hand and, with only the fragile silk between their skins, she could feel the moist warmth of his palm and, against it, the frantic fluttering of her own heart.

When his thumb began stroking across the nipple, it instantly swelled and tightened, straining against him through the silk until her whole self seemed to centre on that taut bud of sensation, and nothing else existed. Dimly, she was conscious of her head arching back, of Nick's mouth, burning-hot now, buried in the soft angle of her neck, of her own wild, shuddering response as she sagged against him——

And then there was a flash of sheet lightning, turning everything dazzling white for an instant, followed directly overhead by a crash of thunder which shook the whole earth. Torn from their private world, they jerked apart, still holding each other, though, and staring tensely into the other's face.

After that one brilliant flash, the darkness was even more intense, but by the single candle-flame Dany saw Nick's expression, his eyes almost black, his face flushed with desire.

Oh, God, what was she doing? As he went to draw her back into his arms, she pushed him away.

'No—no—no!' she burst out wildly and, wrenching herself from his hands, dragged up the neckline of her dress with trembling fingers. The sick shame was coursing through her, turning the raging blood in her veins to ice-cold misery.

'D-don't touch me!' Her voice shook.

'Don't touch you?' His thin lip curled into a sneer as, seemingly back in perfect control of himself, he thrust his thumbs into his jeans belt and lounged back against the door-jamb. 'When you've been asking me to do just that—and plenty more—all evening?'

'Oh.' White to the lips, with mingled self-disgust and anger, Dany took a step back. 'No—no, that's not true. You—— '

'Oh, come on, lady.' He sounded thoroughly bored with the whole proceedings. 'Why the hell else did you put that dress on, if not in some pathetic attempt to seduce me?' And his eyes raked over her slender body with such deliberate contempt that she cringed away.

Was it true? Was that, very deep down, why she'd put on this beautiful—sexy—dress? Not simply to make him eat his words about mini-Tarzans, but for a far less innocent, much darker reason? Whatever the truth of it, she'd allowed him to humiliate her. She longed to fold up at his feet, put her head in her hands and let herself break down into unrestrained sobbing, but from somewhere to her rescue came inner reserves of pride.

Tossing back her dishevelled hair, she said coldly, 'Seduce you? I wouldn't want you making love to me if you were the last man on earth.'

'Ah, of course.' The grating voice flayed her already bleeding nerve-ends. 'Rather late in the day, you've remembered that you have a fiancé.'

As Dany gave a violent start—she hadn't thought of Marcus for hours—Nick reached across and caught hold of her left wrist, dragging up her hand so that she was forced to confront her engagement ring.

'I——' She broke off, the guilty flush staining her cheeks rose-pink.

'But one thing I'll tell you for free, sweetheart.' The harsh, rasping tone made the term of endearment into near-physical abuse. 'From everything I've heard of Medieval Marcus, you'd be one hell of a lot better off in my arms than his.'

Before she could draw back, he released her wrist, letting it drop limply to her side, and drew the back of his hand across her breasts. It was a fleeting touch, doing no more than barely brush the soft flesh through the thin silk, yet without daring to glance down she knew that instantly the nipples had hardened and peaked against him, and knew that he felt it, too.

Just for a second, among the shame and anguish, she saw herself lying in Nick's arms, sated with love, her body and mind filled with him, the taste and touch of him, and felt the slow desire unfurl inside her again.

To crush ruthlessly that hateful vision, she said icily, 'Oh, I don't doubt it.' She paused then went on, choosing her words with stiletto-blade precision, 'After all, they say that lovemaking is an art, don't they?'

He shrugged. 'I've heard it said.'

'Well, you've had so much more practice than Marcus, haven't you, Nick? And you've certainly had more than me. But you see, totally inexperienced as I am—which no doubt makes you despise me all the more—I already know something that you will never know.'

'Really? Do enlighten me.'

'That sex, desire—call it what you like—on its own is worthless. Tenderness, affection and love—they're the things that really matter.' And when he just looked at her, bleak-eyed, she went on defiantly, 'Yes, they're just dirty words in your vocabulary, aren't they?'

No flicker of human warmth lit up those ice-green eyes. 'What a canting little hypocrite you are.'

'No, I'm not. I——'

'Tenderness, affection and love.' His voice was as arid as the wind off the steppes. 'What do you know of any of them?'

'Well, for a start, I love Marcus, so——'

'Correction. You *think* you love him.'

'I don't think—I know I love Marcus,' she hurled back at him, almost weeping with the effect to convince him. 'Very deeply.'

'No, you don't—and I'll tell you why. You see, in all that you've ever said about him, the one thing you show me you don't have is that much——' he snapped his fingers contemptuously '—sexual desire for him. No——' as she tried to interrupt '—you told me what's wrong with me. OK, you're going to listen to what's wrong with you—and listen good. If you loved this man, *really* loved him, desire for him would be so much a part of it that to cut it away would be like cutting your own flesh apart.'

'I do love him!' she cried desperately but, shaking his head, Nick reached out and took hold of her by the shoulders, his fingers digging into her skin.

'No. You're completely untouched—totally unawakened.' He gave her a faintly ironic smile. 'Maybe that's what I wanted to do tonight.'

'S-seduce me, you mean?' She was fighting to keep on the offensive, while she could only hang limply in his arms.

'Not seduce you, no. Timid, completely inexperienced young virgins have very little appeal for me these days.' With cool brutality, he was deliberately scouring the layers of skin from her. 'But in you I feel that there's something—an underlying sensuality—which some man ought to set free, before it's too late.'

'When we're married, Marcus——'

'When we're married.' The lips curved into a bleak, humourless smile. 'When you're married, my dear Dany, you will be trapped in an empty, sterile cage. But don't worry, you won't know about it because by then you'll have been moulded into being just as empty and sterile yourself.'

Dropping his grip, he picked up the candle, his brooding eyes fixed on the flickering flame.

'Just remember this, honey. Those who play with fire are all too often the ones who get burned.' And, thrusting the candle at her, he turned away. 'Go to bed.'

Picking up her skirts, she stumbled past him and on into the sanctuary of the bedroom. She closed the door and leaned against it, her whole body trembling violently until, just before her legs folded like dry straw under her, she tottered over to the bed and sank down on it, her eyes wide and unseeing.

Was he right? Didn't she love Marcus? She drew an unsteady hand across her mouth, her fingers brushing its soft fullness just as his had done. Half fancying that the feel of him still lingered on her skin, she angrily rubbed her lips with the back of her hand to wipe him away, until she winced as a claw from her ring—Marcus's ring—dug into her tender skin.

The tiny circle of candle-light lit up the dress, turning the soft amber to wonderful glowing gold. Why, oh, why had she done it? If only she hadn't worn it, none of this would have happened. They'd have sat out on the veranda, Nick would have given her another chess lesson—he wasn't exactly the world's most patient teacher, but she'd loved that shared intimacy. Now, through her stupidity, she'd shattered once and for all the fragile bond between them. Why hadn't she guessed that, to a highly sexed male animal like Nick Devlin, a woman in a dress like this would be an irresistible provocation?

But was it really her naïveté? Or was it that much more disturbing something deep inside her, which Nick had sensed, leading her out into fathomless waters, where dangerous men like him lay in wait for her to come to them in beautiful, dangerous dresses?

Leaping up, she began ripping open the buttons, frantic now to be out of it. As the silk dropped round her ankles she went to step out of it but then, hearing a faint sound, she spun round to see Nick, lounging in the doorway, arms folded, watching her. His face was quite expressionless, his eyes hooded but, naked except for her white cotton panties, she felt as if his gaze scorched her.

With a strangled gasp, she snatched up her shirt from the bed and held it to her as he straightened up and sauntered across to her, with the insolent grace of a forest cat.

'Don't be alarmed, Ms Trent,' he purred. 'However much it may wound your vanity, I at least am perfectly capable of keeping myself in check. Besides, I've told you before——' the acid in his tone corroded her '——you just aren't my type.'

'Well, that makes us quits, then.'

'But just in case, I came to tell you that you needn't lie awake trembling with terror—or expectation. I shall be sleeping elsewhere. Goodnight—and do sleep well, won't you?'

'Just as well as you will, I'm sure.'

The soft, disbelieving laugh goaded her into even greater anger. Snatching up one of her trainers, she hurled it at the door, but he had already closed it behind him.

A sob was rising in her. She pressed her hand fiercely against her mouth to trap it, then, as the candle wavered and finally died in a little splutter of hot wax, she pulled on her shirt and crawled under the blanket, dragging it up over her head, as she'd used to do when she was a child and wanted to shut out the whole world.

It was almost as though their time at the *hacienda* had never happened. Nick was once more striding out ahead of her, only slowing occasionally to ease the pack on his back, and even then not glancing round to see if she'd been snatched up by a boa constrictor...

Of course, she hadn't been in the least surprised when, after a sleepless night, she'd gone hesitantly to the kitchen and found Nick dressed ready, his rucksack on the table. He didn't even bother to say, 'We're leaving a day early.' Just, 'We only need one pack now—if you fetch that blanket, I'll stow it in here,' and then went on with what he was doing with grim-faced efficiency. But a wave of sheer relief had swept through her...

Now, though, well into the afternoon, despite the fact that she wasn't carrying anything except her bag, Dany's shoulders were bowed down by a weight far heavier

than her pack had ever been—a ton weight
of shame and self-disgust. How could she
have done it—made herself so cheap, humiliating herself in front of a man like him?
She paused for a moment, wiping the back
of her hand across her forehead under the
sticky, sweat-soaked fringe, and gazed at
that forbidding back, marching remorselessly ahead, then set off once more.

Was it the wine that had made her act—
well, so unlike Dany Trent? For that was
the only way to describe it. Or was it the
lush sensuality of the tropical night getting
to her? Oh, come on, she told herself sav-
agely, don't trot out those pathetic excuses.
You wanted him—in fact, you were suf-
fering from an acute attack of sexual desire
for an extremely sexually desirable male.

He'd been right, of course. With one
part of her, at least, she'd known exactly
what she was doing when she'd put on that
dress. Just like that moon moth, she'd been
drawn to a flame. And a man like Nick
Devlin didn't even have to *do* anything—

he just attracted women to their fluttering destruction in the fire.

But that was last night, and now, thank heaven, there were only a few hours to go, and then there would never, *never* be another chance of her so shaming herself with any man. Nick had well and truly taught her that lesson, at least.

Ahead of them the ground rose steeply, as he forced a way through a narrow gulley between two rocky hillsides. They'd been following a stream since early morning, but now they'd climbed above it, and she could only just hear it over her rasping breath. The sky was metallic grey, apart from just ahead, where a bank of evil-looking cloud the colour of overripe damsons lowered over the forest. Even after that mind-blowing thunderclap last night, though, the storm hadn't broken, and now the air was even heavier, more threatening, so that in the torrid heat her clothes were sticking to her. If only it would rain.

And then, quite suddenly, it did. A little gust of wind blew against her face, and next moment the skies opened, throwing out sheeting rain which in seconds had soaked her through.

As she stood, dazed by the speed and force of the downpour, Nick came back, slithering over the wet rocks towards her. His black hair was plastered to his skull, his face streaming. Seizing her arm, he shook it fiercely.

'For God's sake, don't stand there admiring the scenery!' And he began forcing her up the hillside.

'H-how much further?' She could hardly get the words out.

'To the border? Another two hours, I reckon. So cheer up—I told you I'd get you there, didn't I?'

For the first time that day he looked directly at her, his eyes alight with exhilaration, and with a sick lurch of her stomach Dany thought, I don't want those two hours to pass, I don't want to reach the border—I want to stay with him forever.

As the bleak despair flooded through her, there was a rumble from the hillside above. Nick froze, and when she looked up she saw, poised precariously over them on the skyline, a pile of enormous rocks. They hung for a moment then, in agonised slow motion—or so it seemed to Dany's terrified gaze—toppled over the edge and came crashing down, instantly gathering momentum, and the tops of tall trees wavered then disappeared, snapping off like twigs.

Nick stared up one second longer then, seizing her round the waist, he took a diagonal leap off the track and began dragging her bodily across the hillside. From out of the trees a red tide of mud and stones slid like lava, engulfing all in its path. He gave her a final push, then the tide reached them and they were sliding and slipping, the oozing slime sucking horribly round their knees and up to their thighs.

If they once lost their balance... But gradually, still clasping her to him, he fought his way across to a massive logwood tree and, bracing one arm round its trunk, he clamped Dany against him with the other, shielding her with his body. She could feel the spasms running through him as he struggled for breath, his chest heaving. The tree creaked and groaned as its very roots battled for life, then, as the sounds slowly subsided, she opened her eyes and saw across the hillside a hideous red weal, like raw flesh, where moments before there had been green, living forest.

But then, directly overhead, there came another terrifying roar.

'Hell! Another slide—let's get out of here!' Nick yelled. He stood looking round him, peering through the grey wall of rain, then gasped. 'Over there—looks like a cave.' And when she followed his pointing finger she saw, just to their left, a black cleft.

The roar was louder, the rumble of rocks like an earthquake, and as he hauled her across the open ground it shook under their feet. They reached the cave mouth just as the new landslip burst into sight. She slowed momentarily and turned her head, just in time to see the tree which had saved them sway, crack, then go careering down the hillside like a broken matchstick.

'Oh, my darling.' Nick's hold on her tightened even more. 'Don't look like that. We're all right—we're alive!'

He pulled her roughly round to him, and for the space of a single heartbeat they stared into each other's mud-streaked faces. All round them, electricity seemed to spark and crackle as the tensions, not only of the last few terrifying minutes, but all those which had slowly, so very slowly, been building up between them since that very first night in the forest, came to a head. Then the gunpowder ignited and exploded into fiery passion.

There was to be no tenderness. Lost to everything beyond the wild surge of adrenalin through their blood, neither wanted it, neither gave it. Blindly, hands reached out to clasp hands then tear apart, to seek beneath their streaming, mud-caked garments the soft, yielding flesh. At the erotic shock of skin dragging against skin, mouth against mouth, against neck, shoulders, Dany moaned softly, deep in her throat, then, clinging to each other, they were slipping to their knees, in an endless sinking down—down on to the sandy ground.

Nick rolled over, pinning her beneath him, his body taut as a strung bow. Then, as her hips arched to meet his, he drove into her, fiercely, as though he had held himself in check for so long that restraint now was beyond him. As he impaled her with the force of his desire, a tiny gasp broke from her, but he smothered it with his mouth.

Clutching one another's rain-slippery flesh, they began to move, the primitive rhythm building inside them both in an unbearable crescendo until dimly, beyond the thunder of her own heart, Dany heard Nick give a hoarse cry. She felt his whole body tense, and then, with one final thrust, he shattered them both into infinitesimal pieces, and sent them spinning out beyond the cave, the forest, into the black vortex of the universe.

CHAPTER NINE

A MILLENIUM later, Dany felt Nick begin to disengage himself from her arms. When she murmured and tried to hold him close, he shushed her protests with his finger and whispered, 'You're cold. There's some dry wood over there—I'm going to light a fire.'

She lay, eyes half closed, listening to the rain falling outside and Nick moving about in the cave, then, propping herself on her elbow, she watched him. He had wedged his torch into a crack in the rocky wall, and was on his haunches beside a little mound of logs. When he saw her looking he grinned, his teeth white in the half-darkness.

'I knew my Boy Scout training would pay off one day. One of the few things I can remember is how to get a fire going with a couple of twigs.'

As she watched, a faint wisp of smoke came from the kindling, then a spark and finally a tiny yellow flame, which flickered then burst into life as it licked hungrily round the logs which Nick had piled up.

'Where did all that wood come from?'

'Oh, there's a great heap of it back there. I don't somehow think we're the first to use this place as a refuge.' He held out his hand to her. 'Come over here.'

When she sat down beside him he put his arms round her, drawing her to him, then said, 'Your clothes are soaking wet. Get out of them and they'll dry by the fire.'

So she took off her shirt, then her trousers and panties—some of the pretty lace ripped away by the fierce savagery of his lovemaking—so that she was naked, except for the gold chain round her neck. But she felt no shyness of him—that time had long passed. It was as if, in their shared hardship and struggle, they had become very close, needing only this one thing to create a perfect oneness.

He removed his own shirt, then, still holding her with one arm, ripped open the rucksack and pulled out the blanket. Tenderly, he padded her dry then wrapped it round her shoulders as she snuggled against him.

'That better?'

'Mm.' Putting up her hand, she softly brushed her fingertips across his lips, until, catching hold of her hand, he gently kissed the palm.

'My sweet——' his voice was not perfectly steady '——did I hurt you very much?'

'Oh, no—not at all, I promise.' Then, hating the sombre look in his eyes, she went on with a tremulous little smile, 'You were right. It—it was wonderful.'

His fingers tightened on her hand. 'Oh, my——' He broke off, then said, 'Are you hungry? There are a few cans left.'

'No,' she replied softly, 'I'm not hungry. At least, not for—oh, Nick, look.'

Her eyes widening, she gazed round her. The logs were blazing now, and as the flames leapt upwards the walls of the cave gave off a gleaming, molten, red-gold sheen, as if they too were on fire.

Uncoiling himself, Nick went across to the nearest wall, picked at it with his fingernail, then turned to her, his eyes glittering. 'Come and see.'

When she stood beside him, he dropped into her hand a tiny piece of what looked like yellow metal, and she turned it over wonderingly.

'Is it *gold*?'

'No, afraid not—it's a mineral called pyrites. People used to call it fool's gold, though. I suppose because you can't that easily tell it from the real thing.' He reached out and ran his fingers down the gold chain, letting them rest for a moment on the tiny jaguar head which lay in the valley between her breasts.'

'Do you know, Dany——' at the subtle change in his voice, she looked up at him '—in this light, your hair—when I hold it, it flickers and changes from gold to molten fire and back again. It's like a beautiful, living thing.' He had lifted a few strands with his finger, and now let them drift down to her shoulder again.

'And your eyes...' he tilted her face to his, and for once there was no irony, no cynicism, just a great tenderness which tied a hard, tight knot in her chest '...they change colour too. I've watched them...' he might almost have been talking to himself '...seen them darken from topaz to brown and then to gold, as your moods change—or when I kiss you.'

And, lowering his head, he took her full lower lip gently between his teeth and began teasing at it with the tip of his tongue, until a throaty cry was torn from her and she reached blindly for him, her hands clutching, her nails biting into his shoulders.

He swung her up into his arms, carried her back to the fire, still blazing fiercely, then eased the blanket from her and flicked it open on the sand-strewn floor. Very carefully, he laid her down on it, then coming down beside her ran his hands gently down her body so that her breasts stirred instantly into life. Cradling her hips, he buried his face in her belly, his tongue circling round the tiny well of her navel.

Dany was drowning in sensation. 'Let—me—undress—you.' Her voice was slurred with the effort of speaking—of thinking, even—as Nick's hands and tongue drove her nearer and nearer to the edge of wild, unreasoning passion again.

He released her and rolled on to his back. 'I'm all yours.'

But he made no attempt to help her as, her hair tumbling about her face, she tugged off both chestnut leather boots, then put her fingers first to the buckle of the belt round his jeans, then to the zip. Very slowly, frowning in concentration, she pulled the jeans down over his long muscular legs, then paused, her hands at the waistband of his black briefs, to steal a glance at him from beneath her lashes.

He was watching her, the faintest glint of amusement behind those marvellous green eyes and, responding to that secret smile, she swallowed down the last remnants of reserve, took hold of the fragile slip of silk and drew it down.

'You see the effect you have on me?'

Nick's voice was not quite as dry and offhand as he'd intended—she caught the throb of desire behind it, and shook her hair forward to screen her flushed face. He laughed softly, then, reaching up to her, pulled her down beside him, one hand resting on the luscious curve of her hip.

In the leaping firelight, their flesh—hers creamy pale, his sun-bronzed—turned to flame, flickering red and gold, except in the shadowed recesses of their bodies, which were black and limitless as night. As he stroked up her side, the electricity flowed from the ends of his fingers into her, charging her whole frame until every part of her throbbed and tingled.

'You're so warm, so sweet, so achingly soft,' he muttered huskily, 'that I want to plunder all that warmth, bury myself forever in that sweet softness.'

When he took into his mouth, one after the other, her taut, rosy nipples, tasting them, savouring them as though they were some new, unknown delicacy, she gasped out loud, and, clutching her fingers in the thick black hair, crushed his mouth to hers until she felt his teeth bite into her.

A heavy wave of heat rolled through her, leaving her on fire and trembling, and she closed her eyes, but the darkness behind her lids only intensified the scent—the sharply sensual sweat and the lingering muskiness—which clung to her skin and which was Nick Devlin.

When I'm old, she thought with a sudden spasm of anguish, I shall still be able to close my eyes like this, and in the darkness smell the wonderful maleness of a man I haven't seen for fifty years...

And then, as his questing mouth moved lower and lower, over the flat plane of her stomach, she forgot everything beyond the present and the ever more potent feelings he was arousing in her. His fingers brushed against the moist silk of her inner thighs, then, as they sought and found the tiny pulsating core, she gave a gasp of shock and tried to wrench herself free.

But he held her prisoner, so that all she could do was writhe helplessly as he induced in her more and more intense sensations, time after time bringing her to an ever more dizzying peak before drawing her back from the precipice again.

'Nick.' Somehow, she got the one word out.

'Mmm?'

'I—want to please you, too,' she whispered. 'Teach me—everything.'

She felt his smile against her. 'Maybe not quite *everything*—at least, not tonight. Although, I must admit...' raising his head, he gazed down at her in the firelight, his jade eyes gleaming ' ... you do seem an apter pupil at this game than you are at chess. Oh, no, Dany,' as she blushed deeply, 'never be ashamed of your own sexuality—enjoy it.' He blew softly on to her cheek to flick away a strand of tangled hair. 'You were born to be a very sexy lady, you know.'

But only with you, she thought suddenly, with another little twist of anguish. You're the only man who could have awakened this in me—and no one but you will ever be able to assuage it.

'Teach me, then,' she repeated, but had to struggle to keep the desolation out of her voice. 'Do you like this?'

Very softly, she brushed her fingertips over his chest, revelling in the smooth satin feel of his skin, then across the tiny male nipples, feeling them harden instantly.

'And this?' She ran the flat of her hand down over his stomach, feeling the sharp lower edge of his breastbone, and below it the pulse in his stomach, then, lower still, over his belly to the soft dark bush of hair.

'That's enough for a first lesson,' he muttered hoarsely and, rolling her over, came astride her, one knee nudging her legs apart. She reached up to him, gathering him to her, and this time he entered her with infinite slowness, parting the soft folds with such gentleness that Dany all but swooned as her whole body filled with sheer erotic sensation.

When, almost imperceptibly, he began to move, she arched towards him in mute appeal and, as if awaiting her consent, he too arched himself, then drove deeper and deeper. As the flames leapt around them, turning the whole cave into a circle of molten fire, within the blazing ring the flushed, trembling thing that was Dany Trent—muscles, fibres, bones, flesh— slowly melted like candlewax, drop by precious drop, in the flame of his desire, until her whole being was liquid and heavy, molten and white-hot.

Just at the last, he drew himself back, looking down at her, his face set, his eyes the fierce, blazing green of a jaguar about to take and devour its prey, then he spent himself in a meltdown which consumed them both, and Dany, as the flames engulfed her, felt her womb clench then contract, like a fist, then she lay inert and formless beneath him...

Several times, in that short night, she roused, conscious of Nick putting more wood on the fire, and each time, when she turned to him with a little murmur of protest, he gathered her to him, his lips and hands searching and probing in an endlessly new, sweet quest...

When Dany finally woke, the lemon-coloured light of early morning was slanting across the cave mouth. Stretching lazily like a sated cat, as the delicious languor seeped through her limbs, she rolled over. But the space beside her where Nick had lain was empty.

The fire was dead, just grey ashes apart from a few trails of wispy smoke, and Nick, fully dressed, was squatting beside it, his back to her, prodding it with a stick.

'Hi,' she said softly.

He stopped poking at the fire and turned his head briefly. 'Hi.'

But when she smiled, rather tremulously, at him, he did not seem to see the smile, only said brusquely, 'If you want something hot to eat, I can probably get this lot going again.' Another morose prod at the charred sticks.

Dany stared uncomprehendingly at that back for a few seconds, then, in a voice which scarcely seemed to belong to her, said, 'No. No, thanks—I'm not hungry.'

'OK, then. Get dressed, and let's get the hell out of here.' And he gave the fire a final vicious jab so that it collapsed into a lifeless heap, then sprang to his feet.

Dany stared at him a moment longer, then, as he blurred behind a sheen of burning tears, she shivered suddenly— though not from cold—then scrambled to her feet and reached blindly for her clothes. Her trousers and shirt were stiff with mud, but she scarcely noticed as she dragged them on then thrust her feet into her filthy trainers.

She tried just once. As he moved past her towards the cave entrance, she put her hand on his arm.

'Nick.'

He looked down at her hand for a moment as though it were some kind of alien species, then shook himself free, gesturing towards the pack.

'I'm not bothering with that. It's not worth it, now we're so near the border. We'd have made it yesterday if the rain hadn't come.'

She wanted to crawl away into a dark hole somewhere and die.

'Yes, of course.' She was working on automatic pilot, the searing unhappiness burning into her mind like last night's flames. 'Oh—I'll take the blanket, though.'

He frowned, but she was already dropping to her knees. Clumsily, she bundled it together, its bright pattern—like Nick's face—blurring and shifting in front of her eyes, then she slowly straightened up.

He held out a hand. 'Give it me.'

'No!' She clutched it possessively to her. Soon, it would be the only thing left to remind her of their time together, of last night. 'No,' she said again loudly, 'I'll carry it.'

'Suit yourself,' he said laconically, and, turning on his heel, he walked out of the cave.

The sun had just risen over the trees, and in the valley the last of the night's mist was drifting away. Across the hillside, there was the red weal of yesterday's landslip, but soon the forest would have covered it and that reminder of their night here would have gone, too, as ephemeral as the morning mist.

Nick was already striding rapidly up the gully, head down, his hands thrust into his jeans pockets, while his back, square and uncompromising, somehow seemed to shut her out, as she knew it was meant to do. 'I'm a loner...a loner.' Over and over, his bleak words were echoing in her mind. He'd warned her, of course, so she only had herself to blame if she'd allowed herself to hope, deep down, that she might be the single exception. A man like Nick allowed *no* exceptions to his house rules.

You should have known that, you fool, she told herself despairingly.

But last night he'd seemed so tender, so—*loving*.

Yes, but surely you knew that was his technique, tried and tested. He told you that, too. 'I aim to please all of them and leave them happy... But leave is the operative word. I've never met a woman yet for whom, once the passion had cooled, I'd be prepared to give up my freedom.' Well, she had to feel the same.

Far ahead, he reached a rocky incline and paused to look back at her. Sensing the impatience, even at this distance, she hesitated one moment longer then, turning, hurled the blanket back into the cave mouth, in a symbolic little gesture, and went stumbling over the boulders towards him ...

Yet again, he had to wait for her, and as she came up to him along the track they had hit an hour or so back she caught once more that same impatience to be across the border, and free of her once and for all. He tossed away a stick he had been swishing back and forth against his leg.

'You all right?' he asked.

She wanted to fall on all fours in front of him, beating her fists on the ground, and sob, Of course I'm not all right—and you know it, damn you.

Instead, she said through stiff lips, 'Perfectly, thank you—now we're nearly there.' And putting her head in the air, she plunged ahead of him along the track.

He could easily have caught her up, of course, for her pace soon slowed in the sweltering heat, but for the very first time he chose to allow her to go on ahead of him, and that only increased even more the dull ache under her ribs. Aware of nothing beyond that pain and the sound of her lungs, rasping for breath, she plodded on grimly. But then she stopped suddenly.

Just ahead, in a little pile of dead leaves, something had stirred, something was rustling the leaves. She looked down and saw, almost at her feet, a small snake, brilliantly banded in orange, gold and black.

As she stared at the creature, still barely able to focus her thoughts on it, she heard, from just behind her, Nick say softly, 'Don't move.'

She froze, but then, as the snake raised its head a little, straight towards her, a violent push sent her staggering sideways so that she fell heavily among the undergrowth alongside the track. There was one angry, sibilant hiss, which curdled her blood, then silence.

Easing herself up gingerly into a sitting position, she glanced round.

'Thank you —— ' But then her voice died into a gasp of fear as she saw Nick, very pale under his tan, leaning up against a tree as though he needed its support. She leapt to her feet.

'Nick, what is it?' When he just shook his head, she blurted out, 'Oh, God, it didn't bite you, did it?'

But he still made no reply and she clutched at his arm, shaking it. 'What was it?'

'A coral snake.'

'They're not p-poisonous, are they?' Terror had her by the throat now, so that she could hardly speak.

'No—hardly at all.' But the words came out far too quickly. 'And anyway, it was only a young one. All the same, though, I'd better have a look at it.'

He slid down the trunk until he was sitting on the ground, then, taking out his penknife, opened it and began hacking through the leg of his jeans.

'Oh, Nick,' her voice shook, 'if I hadn't gone on ahead—it's my fault.'

He gave her the ghost of a smile. 'So— what's new? Here, you finish it off.'

With shaking fingers, she slashed through the tough denim then dragged it down over his boot. There, just above the knee, was a pair of tiny needle-like puncture marks, and around them the flesh was already swelling, a horrible, livid putty colour.

She stared down at the wound, then, shaking herself free of the panic which was threatening to overwhelm her, jumped up and, dragging her shirt over her head, ripped a length from the bottom of it. Some twigs lay under the canopy of the tree. She chose a straight one, testing it for strength, then knelt down beside Nick, whose eyes were closed.

'Hold that.'

She shook his arm fiercely when he did not respond, then, placing the tourniquet against his thigh, began winding the make-shift bandage round and round above those evil little puncture holes.

'Quite a little Florence Nightingale.'

He grinned at her, but his voice, she realised fearfully, was already slightly slurred as if he had been drinking. But she managed to smile back at him, and said lightly, 'Oh, didn't you know? When you were busy being a Boy Scout, I was getting my Brownies' First-Aid badge.'

But Dany, adder bites aren't at all the same thing as venomous Central American coral snakes...

Thrusting the terrifying thought from her, she finished the tourniquet and began knotting the bandage. 'Can you bear it any tighter?'

'Mmm.' He nodded, and she tightened the end until she saw him wince, the material digging deep into his thigh.

He opened his eyes and looked straight at her. 'You must leave me here—go for help.'

'Leave you? Don't be a fool,' she said roughly.

I'd never get back to you again in time... As the appalling words trembled unspoken on her tongue they stared at each other, then she snatched up her wrecked shirt and pulled it back on.

'You said once, you'd carry me over the border if necessary—well, if necessary, I'll carry you. Now, let me help you up.'

Putting her hands under his arms, she half dragged him to his feet, where he stood, swaying gently, but upright.

'Lean on me. *Yes.*' As he protested, she seized his arm and draped it across her shoulders, then put her arm round his waist.

It was slow and painful. Every step, every fifty metres was an effort. Nick, without an ounce of excess fat on his frame, was a dragging weight, even if he was all bone, sinew and muscle, and very soon Dany could feel her heart pounding against her ribs as the sweat poured off her in rivulets.

She sneaked a sidelong glance at him. He was ash-pale, his eyes three-quarters closed. She thought of the poison, seeping little by little through his veins, nearer and nearer to his heart, then swallowed down the terror, and forced herself on...

Time became meaningless. Only his tremendous will-power was keeping him on his feet—most men would have crumbled long since. And then, very slowly, he folded up and slid through her clutching hands on to the ground.

Dany threw herself on her knees beside him, frantically cradling his dark head to her breast. All vestige of colour had gone from his face; there was a film of sweat on it and through the all but closed lids she could see those beautiful jade eyes, all the life going from them.

'Nick!'

But when she shook him, he only muttered irritably and turned his cheek to her breast, like a sleeping child. She stared down at him, gnawing her lip, until she tasted the blood, fighting against the terrible sob of anguish that was ripping her apart inside, then she shook him again.

'Don't die, damn you! I won't let you— do you hear me? I love you.'

And she knew suddenly that it was true. She loved this man with all her being—and he was dying in her arms.

Raising herself first to her knees then upright, she took hold of him again and began slowly, painfully, dragging him along the path. Count to a hundred, she told herself, and you'll be there...and two hundred...and four hundred...

The noise roused her. She gazed up, blinking the sweat from her eyes, and saw, though she barely registered it, that at some time in the distant past they had emerged from the track and were on a wide dirt road. The noise was louder now, and she saw, coming towards them through a cloud of orange dust, a battered jeep.

Letting Nick's inert body fall, she sprang in front of it, and even before it squealed to a halt she was at the driver's door, tugging at him.

'*Señor* —' But her little Spanish had gone in a cloud of fear and exhaustion, and she just pointed to Nick.

The driver and another man, both in khaki uniforms, knelt by him. They looked at each other, she caught the word '*serpiente*', and then he was being lifted gently into the back...

One of the men was speaking to her, holding her by the arm, asking if she was all right. Then, even as she smiled at him through lips which belonged to someone else, she felt herself keeling over into the blackness which was rushing to engulf her.

'Dany.'

From a very long way away, someone was calling her name. She stirred, opened her eyes, and saw, leaning towards her in the cool half-dark——

'Gramps? Is—is that you?' she murmured muzzily.

'Hello, my pet.' Her grandfather bent and kissed her cheek, then took her hand between his. 'How are you?'

'Oh, I'm fine.' She yawned and stretched.

'Well enough to get a good scolding?' He gave her a meaningful look from beneath shaggy brows, and she flushed guiltily.

'I'm sorry, Gramps—for worrying you, I mean.' She sank back on the pillows, looking around her. She was lying in a metal-frame bed in a whitewashed room, a ceiling fan whirring softly overhead. 'Where am I?'

'The local hospital. The embassy sent for me two days ago.'

'Two days!' The haze of sleep finally cleared from her brain, and she clutched at his hand. 'Nick. H-how is he? Have you seen him?'

'Briefly.'

Thank God. So he wasn't—she pushed the ugly word away from her. 'W-what did he say?'

'Not a great deal.' He paused. 'You realise you saved his life?'

'Oh.' She shrugged. 'Well, he saved mine—several times over. Anyway, he's all right.'

She lay back again, but a faint frown still creased her brows. 'You know, Gramps, I had an awful dream. I dreamt that I got up and went to find him—and he was next door; he had tubes in his arm, and there were men in white coats bending over him—and then one of them saw me and came out and carried me back to bed.'

Her grandfather nodded. 'That's right. He's called Dr Mendoza.'

She gaped up at him. 'You mean it wasn't a dream? I really went?'

'Well, sleep-walked would be a better description, from what they told me,' he replied drily.

'When can I see him?' she asked eagerly, but then his expression changed, sending a spasm of fear right through her.

'Dany, my dear——'

'*No!* He's all right—you said he's all right.' Pushing back the thin counterpane in a violent gesture, she sat up and swung her legs over the edge. 'I'm going to see him now.'

'Don't, Elly. You're not strong enough yet.'

She stared at him, as though she hardly saw him. Elly—the childish name he hadn't used for years. And suddenly, she knew. Nick was dead—that was the terrible truth they were trying to keep from her.

'No, Gramps.'

She stood up, swaying slightly in the voluminous cotton nightie, and, gently disengaging her hand from his, went out on to the shady veranda. She knew the way— she'd been there before, hadn't she, in that waking nightmare when Nick had lain, white and still?

Pushing open the door, she went in, then stopped. Two women in striped dresses were stripping off the bed, and a young nurse—a nun—was disconnecting some apparatus alongside it. An involuntary sound was torn from Dany's throat; the nurse turned sharply then came to her.

'Señorita Trent.'

'Nick—Mr Devlin—where is he?' Her pale mouth, stiff with the unbearable terror which gripped her whole body, could barely get the words out. 'Is he——?'

She stopped. She must go on refusing to say the word, and that way she could make it not true. Because it mustn't be—she couldn't bear it, not to live the rest of her life knowing that somewhere on the earth he was waking, smiling, laughing...

The nun's smooth young face creased with concern. 'But, my dear child, Señor Devlin left early this morning. Dr Mendoza tried to persuade him, but he insisted on discharging himself. He was flying to the States, I believe, but I can check on that if you —'

'No—no, thank you.'

At the kind concern in the nun's face, Dany heard her own voice tremble. Somehow, she managed a ghostly smile, then, turning, went back to her own room.

Her grandfather was standing looking out of the window, but when she sank down on the side of the bed he muttered something then, coming across, sat down beside her and put his arm round her, pulling her to him so that her head rested on his broad shoulder.

'Dany —' he cleared his throat '—Dany, Nick's a great chap—I'd trust him with my life in a tight spot. That's why I got him to keep an eye on you. But —' he cleared his throat again '—he didn't— er—harm you in any way, did he?'

She stiffened and looked up at him. Then, at the unhappiness in his face, she somehow pulled herself back a few paces from that black hole of misery she was sliding into.

'Oh, no, Gramps, Nick took very good care of me. He didn't harm me at all.'

Well, only my heart—that's cracked into a million pieces. But, somehow, I'll stick them all back together again, she silently added.

CHAPTER TEN

'ARE you sure you're all right now, Dany?'

'Yes, I'm fine, thanks, Caroline.'

'Mmm.' The other woman pursed her lips. 'You're still very pale and washed out. You should have stayed home another day. Anyway, what did the doctor say?'

'Oh, you know.' Dany was evasive. 'Maybe it's just that I haven't got over that heavy cold—or it's winter-itis setting in early, and all I need is a week in the sun, et cetera.'

'Could be.'

But her employer was still eyeing her dubiously, and, to try to divert her, Dany said hastily, 'I'll finish polishing those Georgian spoons I left the other day.'

'It's all right, I did them myself yesterday.'

'Well——' Dany looked round the up-market antique shop, then hurriedly crossed to the display cabinet which held the choicest pieces of jewellery '—I'll re-arrange these rings.'

But it was only one of the rings that held her gaze, as it always did. The most expensive in the shop, the huge tawny gold stone, in a heavy, dark gold setting, was superb...

'With eyes like yours, you should have a ring with a huge tawny topaz...' Was there always going to be, every day—every hour of every day of her life—a stabbing reminder of Nick...?

'No,' her boss said firmly. 'What you're going to do is take the rest of the afternoon off. Go home and put your feet up. No arguments,' as Dany protested feebly. 'We're slack at the moment, but by the end of the month I'm going to need you fit and on your feet for the pre-Christmas rush.'

'Well, if you're quite sure.' Dany, the tight band round her head tightening notch by notch, was weakening.

'Or why don't you call off at that exhibition you were telling me about? It finishes tomorrow, and you keep saying you ought to go.'

Outside, the early October afternoon was chilly. Dany buttoned up her royal-blue jacket against the swirling wind and pulled on her leather gloves. As she walked off down the quiet street, that black shadow which always stalked her, and which she only kept at bay by being among people, leapt out at her, sending waves of stark misery through her so that she faltered in her stride.

And today was even worse... That visit to the doctor, which had only confirmed what deep down she'd known for weeks... She'd have to tell Gramps soon, and Caroline—though even if she didn't, her boss's eagle eye would spot the truth any day now.

She came to where her route divided—one way the Tube station, the other, the museum—and she stood gazing listlessly into space. She didn't want to go to the exhibition—Gramps had tried to persuade her to go to the official opening, but she'd fought against it—but she didn't want to go back to her bed-sit either, to spend yet another evening staring at the opposite wall. And perhaps if she made herself go, to confront her pain head-on, it might even be the one thing that could exorcise it and start her on the road back to being alive.

The exhibition was in a side gallery—the stark black lettering announced 'Threatened Treasures of the Rain Forests', and the name of the United Nations organisation which was sponsoring it on its fund-raising tour round the world. She fumbled in her bag for money for a catalogue, then went in, the swing door closing behind her.

Immediately, she heard the soft music. It was native Indian, mainly reed pipes, a strangely melancholy, haunting quality about it that brought sudden tears to her eyes. The last time she'd heard music like this had been at that folk evening at the hotel—just three nights before she'd gone out into the forest, met Nick Devlin, and ruined her happiness forever.

Around her on the walls, as a prelude to the exhibition, were huge monochrome photographs. She glanced idly at them, and next moment her heart gave a little skitter. There, surely, was the pyramid she'd stumbled on—that huge gaping hole ripped into its entrails. There were several shots of it, each one more dramatic than the previous, but all subtly conveying the savage greed which had ravaged its decaying splendour.

Had Nick taken them? Perhaps. But this one he hadn't taken—for here he was, kneeling by that clump of bamboo, the wrecked plane in the background. The turf was dug away and he was holding up one of the painted pottery bowls. She stared into that face, as though to conjure him off the two-dimensional paper. He was smiling faintly, but otherwise his face was inscrutable—though surely round the mouth and eyes strain showed.

She stood in front of it for a long time, but then, conscious of the attendant's discreet eye on her back, moved on into the main exhibition. It was superbly staged, the lighting subdued so that the illuminated display cases seemed to float against the darkness. There were dozens of pottery items, among them some which she was sure were from the hoard in the plane, then several cases of silver and alloy objects, which she didn't recognise, and then, at the far end, the most precious items.

There were the golden butterflies, brought at the *conquistadores'* command to ransom a king, now pinned to black velvet. And next to them—yes, it was the goddess of fertility, her belly swollen, holding the child and the ear of corn. Barely aware of what she was doing,

Dany's own hands moved to cradle the soft curve of her abdomen through the wool jacket.

And suddenly, with a little sunburst of joy which cut right through the grey unhappiness, she thought, Nothing matters, really, beside this wonderful, marvellous child we made together. She'd never see Nick again, but her love for him was like a tiny flame, lit by the leaping fire in that molten cave, and if she let it, all her life, through the lonely bleakness, it would warm her.

Apart from the attendant, perched on his stool, she'd had the room to herself, but now, hearing the swing doors open and close softly, she hurried on to the final case. It contained just one item. On a bed of black velvet lay the gold chain. There was the carved jaguar head, the lips curled in a snarl, the jade-green eyes staring back at her.

She looked up from those eyes and saw, out of the darkness on the other side of the case, another pair of jade-green eyes watching her.

'*Nick*?'

A wave of dizziness went through her, and she put a hand up to her head. He came swiftly round to her and, putting his arm round her, gave her a rather crooked grin.

'Sorry to give you a fright.'

His arm felt wonderful—warm and alive and strong. She jerked away from it.

'Don't worry. It was just seeing you like that, I suppose.' She marvelled inwardly at her composed tone, and felt brave enough to go on. 'Quite a coincidence, our both being here.'

Another tight smile. 'Not really. Tom gave me the address of that antique shop, and the owner—Caroline?—said you'd either gone home or here. She also said she'd sent you home early because you aren't well.'

He eyed her and, terrified of what his scrutiny would reveal in her face, she pulled back from him and said coolly, 'Oh, no, I'm fine.' But when he looked at her, brows raised in patent disbelief, she blurted out, 'What have you come for, Nick? What do you want?'

'Well—I never did get around to thanking you for saving my life, did I?'

Dany, her hands clenched in her pockets, forced a careless shrug. 'You saved mine too, I seem to remember.'

'And...' there was a wholly new hesitancy in his voice '...how's Marcus?'

'Marcus? What about him?'

She tried to look him straight in the eye, but it was very difficult. That face, which she'd seen so often in her dreams, was so close that all she had to do—ached to do— was reach out and caress it. Instead, she jammed her hands even further into her pockets.

'I asked Tom, when I rang him, if you were married. He told me—fairly bluntly——' the thread of irony was a glimmer of the old Nick '—that if I wanted to know I could ask you myself.'

Without warning, he reached for her left arm, and gently, but inexorably, drew out her hand then slowly pulled off the glove. He looked down at the fingers, bare of any rings, and, knowing him so well, Dany sensed him relax a fraction.

'That's right,' she said, in a brittle voice. 'I gave it back to him.'

'Was it——?' He stopped.

'Because of us, you mean?' she replied expressionlessly. 'Yes. But I think he was secretly relieved. While I was away, he——'

'Finally realised just what he was taking on,' he completed for her, a faint glint of laughter in his voice.

'Probably.' But she wouldn't respond, wasn't going to smile or laugh with him. That would let him in again, near enough to break her heart all over again, just when she'd managed to fix a few of the pieces together. And, above everything else, she mustn't let him guess about the baby—she couldn't bear his pity or his duty-bound offers of help.

A group of students burst in, chattering like starlings, and he grimaced. 'Look, if you've finished here——?'

'Yes, I've seen all I wanted to.'

Outside on the pavement they stood, jostled by the early rush-hour commuters. Turning to him, she put out her hand like a polite child.

'Goodbye, Nick. It's been——'

He pushed the hand aside. 'I haven't come three thousand miles just to say goodbye in five minutes flat.'

She stared at him. 'You mean you really did come to London to see *me*?'

'Why the hell else would I cancel a sailing trip round the Bahamas I've been looking forward to for months? Come and have tea with me.'

'No—no, I don't want to.'

She took a step back from his restraining arm, and he scowled. '*Yes*—and just for once, Danielle Trent, you're going to do as I tell you.'

He put up a finger and, as from nowhere, a taxi glided in alongside them, he opened the rear door and gave her a smart shove.

'Where to, sir?'

'The Savoy.'

Leaning back, Nick gazed out of the side-window. Dany, though, sat staring straight ahead, her arms folded defiantly, but then, unable to keep her eyes from him any longer, she risked a sidelong glance.

When she'd last seen this man—apart from that nightmare vision in the hospital—he'd been filthy, unkempt, his jeans ripped half off him. Now, he was in a pale grey suit which oozed 'designer' from every stitch, white silk shirt, navy tie, and an off-white trenchcoat, the sleeve of which, as the taxi rounded a sharp bend, brushed against her bare hand, so that she withdrew it quickly.

And yet the basic nature of the man hadn't changed one iota. After those first few moments of uncertainty—brought on, presumably, by some vague feelings of guilt—he was exactly the same, exuding from every pore a kind of sleekly feral quality, and that same barely contained impatience to be active. As the cab revved at traffic-lights, she watched his hands beat an irritable tattoo against his knee—that hand, those lean, tanned fingers, which, within that circle of fire, had caressed her into mindless oblivion . . .

'We can't talk here.' A babble of voices and the clatter of china met them, and Nick turned away towards the lifts. 'We'll have tea in my suite.'

In the lift, he was still silent, staring at the floor, and when Dany sneaked another look at him her heart sank. Moody, morose—nothing had changed. He must have known how she felt about him, so in that case why had he done it—elbowing his way back into her life, as if deliberately to cause her more pain? She ought to be angry—and yet all she wanted to do was take him in her arms and with her fingertips gently stroke away the lines of strain and tension...

When the tea-trolley was wheeled in, she remained at the picture window, gazing out past the lights of London springing up against the early evening sky.

'Milk? Sugar?'

She turned slowly. 'Milk, please—no sugar.'

He poured her tea, then patted the sofa beside him, but she took the armchair opposite.

'Sandwich?' He pulled back a corner of the bread. 'Cucumber. What else, in England?'

'Naturally.' She smiled faintly, but inside her the depression was welling up in a black wave.

He glanced down at the delicate, wafer-thin bone china. 'Slightly different from ——'

'Why did you leave without saying goodbye?'

Their eyes met—for the first time since they had left the exhibition—then he said slowly, 'But I did. It's just that I'd made sure you were still out to the world, so's you wouldn't hear me as I stood at your bedside. And then ——' He broke off.

'And then?'

'I got the hell out of it,' he said bleakly. 'Just as far and as fast as I could go.'

'I see.' She gave him a small, sad smile.

'No, you don't see.' He banged down his cup. 'You don't see at all—and neither did I for weeks. I even succeeded in half convincing myself that it was for your own good that I'd beat it, that I had no regrets. Even that, for just once in my life, I was doing the big self-sacrifice thing and letting Marcus back in, instead of a cynical, world-weary guy who never tired of telling

any woman who'd listen what a wonderful, self-sufficient lover he was——'

He broke off abruptly again, then, 'For
God's sake, come and sit beside me——' he
shot her a glinting smile '—*please*, Ms
Trent.'

When she sank down beside him on the
plush sofa—but not too close—he reached
for her hand and held it between his.

'Do you still love me, Dany?' He spoke
so softly that she scarcely heard the words.

'You know I do,' she said simply, and
when he turned her face to his she smiled
tremulously at him. 'There's no point in
lying, is there?'

'Not really.' He brushed her lips gently
with his thumb. 'It was just my own
feelings I wasn't so sure about.'

What was he trying to tell her? 'But you
don't even think I'm all-woman.'

'So I remember telling you.' He gave her
a rather frayed smile. 'I was fool enough
to think that if I said it often enough I'd
come to believe it myself. There you were,

under my charge, engaged to another man—whom I would dearly have loved to tear apart with my bare hands—and you the most desirably feminine female I have ever met.'

'Oh, Nick.' She bit her lip as, tentatively, her splintered heart began to mend.

'And I reckon I'd have made it, too, if it hadn't been for that landslide——' he gave a self-deprecating grin '—the greatest feat of self-denial since Odysseus and the Sirens.'

'But after—that night...' a delicate blush coloured her pale cheeks '...you were——'

'Such a swine?' He squeezed her hand between his so hard that she almost cried out. 'A massive dose of guilt, honey, for betraying Tom's trust in me. But no—it was more than that.'

And when she looked at him wonderingly he went on jerkily, 'I'm the guy who always walks away with no regrets, remember. Well, with you it was different—

from day one. You took over my life, so that all I could feel, all I could think of was you—and the more I told you that you weren't my type, the more I knew you were the woman I'd been looking for all my life. I wanted to tease you, to make you laugh, to comfort you when you were sad, and so—because I was never going to get involved—I walked away. And I stayed away.'

'So—why did you come back now?'

'Because two nights ago I went to bed drunk—again. Bourbon's gone up on the stock market a notch or two lately.' He gave her a rueful smile. 'And I woke up knowing that I couldn't blot it out any more—I had to know if you were married.'

He reached over to his trenchcoat, which he had tossed across the sofa arm, fished out a small package and dropped it into her lap.

'I saw this back in that place where you're working—and decided to take a chance.'

Dany opened it, and inside, in a nest of white satin, was the topaz ring, in its setting of heavy antique gold.

'Oh—it's so beautiful,' she said breathlessly.

He tilted her face to his, and at his expression her heart lurched. All he said, though, was, 'Just as I'd said—perfect to match those wonderful eyes.'

Seizing her hand, he crushed the ring into her palm. 'You will marry me, won't you, Dany? Tell me yes, before I go quite crazy.'

Yet, even now, something held her back. 'But—you hardly know me.'

'Hardly know you? My darling girl, I've lived so close to you, I know your very heart and soul. I know you're cussed and stubborn and infuriating—but I also know that you are brave and honest and true. Besides, I think I fell in love with you before I even met you.'

'H-how could you have?' She could hardly speak now for happiness.

'The picture that Tom showed me when he was doing his hard sell—the picture of a beautiful girl with red-gold hair and topaz eyes—that was what persuaded me to take you on. I thought then it was just for a few days, but now I'm asking you to take *me* on for the rest of our lives.'

She gave him a blurred smile. 'Yes, Nick, I'll marry you.'

'Oh, my darling.' He slid the ring on to her engagement finger then held her hand, looking down at it, a strange expression on his face. 'What a fool I've been,' he said softly. 'I chose to think that it was just pyrites—fool's gold—I had in my possession, and all the time it was the real thing.' He buried his mouth in her palm. 'Oh, God, Dany, I don't deserve to have you.'

'Of course you do.'

With her free hand, she caressed the top of his head, running her fingers through the black hair, but then, without warning, he sprang to his feet, pushing to one side the tea things, which they had barely touched. Going across to the fridge, he opened it and peered inside, then took out a bottle of champagne.

'Well, well!' he exclaimed. 'Bollinger '79.'

Opening it, he poured out two glasses, then came back to sit by her. He handed her a glass.

'Well, Dany—to us.'

'To us.' But then she remembered, and her heart, so nearly whole again, gave a painful jolt. 'Oh—Nick.'

'What is it?' As she set down her glass, the contents untasted, he looked at her sharply. 'What's wrong?'

'Maybe before I say yes——'

'Well?' he broke in impatiently.

'You may change your mind.' She made a pale attempt at a teasing smile.

'Just *tell* me—or do I have to shake it out of you?'

And so, unable to tell him in words, she took his hand and laid it across her abdomen, its gentle swell still all but invisible beneath her blue and green Paisley wool dress.

As he looked at her, his eyes blank with shock, she said quietly, 'I'm having a baby, Nick.'

'A baby? You mean *my* baby?' He sounded stunned. 'That night in the cave?'

She nodded.

'Well, why the hell didn't you tell me— write me as soon as you knew? No—*don't* tell me.' Very pale, he raked his fingers through his hair. 'You were afraid that, having let you down once, I'd take off even harder in the opposite direction if I saw you coming with my baby in your arms. Well— was that it?'

'Something like that, I suppose,' she said, almost inaudibly, her head bent so that she would not have to see the rejection in his eyes. Any moment, he was going to start edging away, tell her, Sorry, honey. You can hold on to the ring as a keepsake, of course, but otherwise——

'Oh, my darling love,' Nick said, in a funny, choked voice, and gathered her into his arms, his cheek against her soft hair.

'And you'll never go—never walk away from me again, I mean? I couldn't bear that.' Her voice was muffled against his jacket, but he heard her.

'My sweet——' he held her away from him to give her a lop-sided grin '—I'm just terrified that one day you'll discover what an arrogant, moody, unbearable swine I am——'

'Oh, I discovered that long ago.' But when she gave him a provocative look from under her lashes he could not respond to it.

'And walk away from me,' he continued, 'when all I want in life is you. I want to have you—and our children—beside me. I want to grow old with you beside me.'

'Well—here I am.'

And as Dany held out her arms Nick drew her tenderly into his embrace, his lips telling her that all she had yearned for in the past weeks was hers. And more, infinitely more, besides.

MILLS & BOON NOW PUBLISH
EIGHT LARGE PRINT TITLES A MONTH.
THESE ARE THE EIGHT NEW TITLES
FOR NOVEMBER 1992

———————— ✳ ————————

FEELINGS OF LOVE
by Anne Beaumont

STORMFIRE
by Helen Bianchin

CAVE OF FIRE
by Rebecca King

THE ORCHARD KING
by Miriam Macgregor

DANGEROUS SANCTUARY
by Anne Mather

ROMANTIC ENCOUNTER
by Betty Neels

INTRIGUE
by Margaret Mayo

NO PROVOCATION
by Sophie Weston

MILLS & BOON NOW PUBLISH
EIGHT LARGE PRINT TITLES A MONTH.
THESE ARE THE EIGHT NEW TITLES
FOR DECEMBER 1992

———————— * ————————

REVENGE
by Natalie Fox

PAST LOVING
by Penny Jordan

YESTERDAY AND FOREVER
by Sandra Marton

WINTER OF DREAMS
by Susan Napier

THE FINAL SURRENDER
by Elizabeth Oldfield

MORE THAN A DREAM
by Emma Richmond

CATALINA'S LOVER
by Vanessa Grant

OUT OF NOWHERE
by Patricia Wilson